THE AWAKENED
Warriors Rising

Andrea Campbell
Haruto Iwasaki

ISBN: (e-book) 978-9-464-98691-4

ISBN: (Paperback) 978-9-464-98690-7

Front cover and other art by Lee Sneyers

Book design by Lee Sneyers

Distributed by:

Lulu

First printing edition 2024.

Publisher: Bell publishing (Andrea Campbell and Lee Sneyers)

www.theawakened.be

For Lee.

Without you this book would not have happened.

Thank you for your ideas, patience, and tireless support of our work.

Breeland
DJANIA
Ypare
ROMINORE
KNETT
Jinorial

Mecodor
Islands

Prancinia

Thaedim

Eternal Garden

Mendani

Kilgaris

Nüland

EMAICH
Wanyd Clan

Grantan

Redall

TOKAREI
Veronn Clan

LIUNIA
Frithe Clan

Kanera

N

RANINALE

Table of Contents

THE AWAKENED

Warriors Rising

Andrea Campbell
Haruto Iwasaki

PROLOGUE

Robyn’s feet splashed into the shallow water, hitting land.

It had been three days at sea in her small motorboat, but she'd landed on Nüland just as she ran out of supplies.

She reached into her boat for some rope and towed it to shore. If she was correct, she'd be back home in just a few more days. She had avoided the major harbours where cargo ships docked and the smaller marinas, where yachts and leisure boats mostly slept. She'd navigated to a quiet beach where no one would notice her return. She was highly aware of how illegal her voyage had been.

She was one of the last of a warrior clan that had led the victory against Thaedim.

Robyn's family still trained in the old ways, and she had just returned from a year alone in Thaedim to complete her training, as everyone in her family did. She excelled at close combat, and her speed allowed her to usually defeat an enemy before they knew what had happened. This had saved her life many times over the past year. But she hadn't had a full night's sleep either. She wondered if this was what early parenting felt like.

Once she'd pulled her boat to shore, she sat in the sand, considering what to do next. She absentmindedly reached into her pack and pulled out some herbs she'd collected on Thaedim, as well as a grinder. She could go back to her family and continue within the confines of clan life, or she could turn her back on all that and embrace the new society.

Not ready to face her next step, Robyn stayed on the beach a little while longer and watched the sun come up as she ground the benthe herbs into a fine powder for tea.

PART 1 - ALLIANCES

1

Grantan, Hunter

Present day, the year 6103

“Is that suitcase gonna be big enough?” Hunter asked sarcastically.

“I’m going for a year: that’s all 4 seasons. I’ve gotta be prepared.” Gina’s suitcase was lying on the floor of her room, it was half full.

“I guess, but can’t you get stuff there?”

“Ypare is a small town; I don't think they'll sell human clothes on every corner.”

“Fair enough, but the toffee squares?”

“What have you got against toffee? It’s non-perishable!” She protested.

“I guess.” Hunter sat as he watched the chaotic process that was his best friend’s packing style.

Gina closed the first suitcase in triumph.

“Just five more days! I can’t wait to board an airship. They say that the airship journey lasts three days. I get to ride an airship! I don’t get to see Prancinia this time, I’ll have to go straight to Ypare to meet my supervisor – uh…” she looked at a piece of paper on her desk “Brtann…Br-TANN… BRtann…?”

Hunter could see her making a mental note to figure out the pronunciation before meeting him.

Hunter shrugged, "You're the one who speaks Djanian, not me." He thought for a moment and then looked up from where he was sitting. "Maybe I'll go on an adventure too."

"Sure, why not?"

"I've never been to Redall, even though my mom lived there for a while before I was born. I think it's time I check it out. And then there's my mom's stories about Thaedim. Maybe I'll try my luck there. Who knows? Maybe I'll find out that I'm the Awakened. Hah!"

"I'm ok with part A of that plan, part B doesn't sound so great. You know the Treaty made it so the demons can never leave the island. That's how dangerous they are to us. Why would you want to go there?"

"Well, Grandpa never stops talking about how I can only be a real warrior if I train on Thaedim."

"Why on Nüland would you want to be a warrior!? There's no future in that unless you want to join the thug-like cops."

"I'd make a pretty good thug cop." Hunter laughed.

Gina groaned, "No argument here."

"On the other hand, *you* get to be a Djanian Outreach Coordinator, how can you say that with a straight face?" Hunter said, chuckling again.

"Shut up: it's what I trained for in university. This is my dream job. I wonder if there is anything like the Djanian markets we have here? Can you imagine the accessories?" Gina sighed happily.

Hunter threw a pillow at her with surprising force.

Gina grunted as it hit her in the stomach.

"Enough gloating. Are you ready to take a break? You've been at this forever."

"Fine, fine. Let's go get coffee. And maybe we can stop at the Djanian market on the way back."

"Gina, come on. You'll be in Djania later this week; can't you look at that stuff when you're there?"

"Ok," Gina conceded and got ready to leave with Hunter.

Five days later, Gina boarded the airship. Hunter stood at the launch site, with the other family and friends seeing people off. He looked up at the sky and watched as the ship got smaller and smaller in the distance.

"Goodbye, Gina," he said to himself. She was his only friend with mixed heritage: a mother from Tokarei, a father from Raninale. And the tell-tale darker skin tone and hair colour that made that heritage clear. A sharp loneliness swept over him.

A few days later, Hunter found himself at home again, going through the same routines. He was bored. At 20, he'd trained for 12 years to become a Veronn clan warrior, but had never been in an actual fight. The treaty that had ended the Thaedim War had been signed nearly a hundred years ago, and he could see that the warrior clans were transitioning into business to stay relevant and were losing the link to the old ways. It had been on his grandpa Neil's insistence and willingness to occupy himself with the training that Hunter had followed the old warrior training.

He hadn't been joking when he'd mentioned becoming Awakened to Gina, he wanted to be the one in his family that could access the once-in-generations power that his clan possessed.

But now, nearly four generations since the war had ended, the clan's powers had not resurfaced. Hunter was beginning to think that he needed to get away and experience the world.

In the Thaedim War, it had initially just been warriors and magic users that joined the war, but soon all coastal countries on Nüland had been drawn in. Only Raninale, deep in the south, had escaped. Warriors and magic users from across the continent had flocked to the coast and established the four clans: Veronn, Wanyd, Strannae, and Frithe to fight the demons. Eventually, magic users and regular humans fought side-by-side with the support of Djania. The Djanians had kept the demons at bay for generations before humans entered the war.

About a week after Gina's departure, Hunter approached his parents.

"I'm thinking about taking an extended trip, kinda like the one you took at my age," he said, nodding towards his mom, "I was thinking to start in Redall and then maybe do my final training in Thaedim."

"What about Raninale? There's lots to see there." Hunter's dad suggested.

Hunter shrugged, "Maybe next time dad. I think I want to make this a warrior trip."

"Suit yourself" his dad replied. His dad's easy-going nature was completely at odds with his talent as a goldsmith. When he was in the Veronn clan forges enhancing their swords, his focus and intensity appeared. The same focus and intensity that could be seen in Hunter as he practised his sword fighting. He turned to his mom.

"If this is something that you need to do, I can't stop you. But a word of caution: just because you are still on the human continent doesn't mean there aren't any threats. You will need to be just as guarded in Redall as you will on Thaedim."

Hunter was surprised. His mom was tough. She could still spar with him, and despite his greater strength, he was often beaten by her strategic approach and experience. The fact that she saw equal threats in both places gave him pause, but not for long.

Hunter began his planning; his small savings from a few part-time jobs added up to about a month that he could comfortably travel for and, if he budgeted correctly, maybe two months.

When he was packing, an envelope appeared on the pile of clothes he'd set out. He said a silent thank you to his parents for this extra boost to his financial situation. Without a second thought, he shoved it in his pack and continued his preparations to leave.

2

Ypare, Gina

After a complicated mix of airship and high-speed light rail that had taken nearly five days, Gina surveyed her new home on the other side of the planet. She'd known, in theory, what she was signing up for when she took on this post, but the reality was different. She'd left the light rail far behind and now stood at a rickety train platform that seemed about to fall apart.

Two large suitcases and a backpack were all she'd brought with her to see her through this year abroad. As she stood on the platform another one-car train, exactly like the one that she'd just gotten off from, was pulling into the station. Gina was mildly surprised to see another train arrive so soon after hers. The station did not seem to be a hub of activity.

A few locals stepped out, and Gina realised how strange she must look to them. Humans evolved as the dominant species in the south-eastern continent, Nüland, and breesians dominated the north-western continent, Breeland. The island Thaedim stood between the two major landmasses and was home to a variety of different species, which humans had lumped together under the category of demon. Breesians, like humans, had evolved to be bipedal, but maintained body fur and a tail. They had a heightened sense of hearing and smell, their legs were reverse jointed, making them quicker and more agile on foot, but their hands were much less developed, leading them to develop gauntlets that would compensate for this evolutionary weakness. Humans and breesians had tentative relations now, despite the close allyship in the Thaedim War.

Because of the war, there was quite a diaspora on both sides. In larger human cities, Djanians had established breesian communities and many humans lived in the Djanian capital Prancinia. Of all the three breesian nations, Djania was by far the most well-known to humans because of their technological development and role alongside humans in fighting against Thaedim. Djania was making efforts to bridge the cultural gaps with humans for their mutual benefit. Gina had been born in a mid-sized city, Grantan, where she had encountered Djanians since childhood, and her fascination with them had led her to study their language, history, and culture. After she graduated university, she'd been hired by Denma Corp because of her degree. Although her practical experience was lacking, her Djanian studies had been extensive.

This far into the countryside, there were few non-breesians. The local people followed the trends from the big cities with brightly coloured clothes and accessories that Gina couldn't help but focus on. Like all breesians, they had slightly leopard-like facial features, with long, pointed ears that were much more sensitive than Gina's. But their sight was less developed than that of humans. Breesians were taller on average than humans, but they rarely used their size to intimidate.

The locals stared at her, noses twitching; they didn't approach.

Two began a conversation in the local dialect, a low guttural sound that Gina had been studying in the months leading up to her arrival. Since the shape of their mouths and vocal cords were so different from hers, there was only limited progress that she could hope to make. Though breesians, when born abroad, seemed to be able to develop the adaptations necessary to speak Nülandish fluently.

They also communicated in ways she couldn't, especially through sounds that she was not capable of hearing, and also with their tails. Before arriving, her company had offered a simulator experience where she could experience reality the way the breesians did. With heightened hearing and limited vision, she'd experienced the incredible agility but limited strength and range of motion in their hands.

She had some understanding of what they must think of this short, mostly hairless human. But, at least, Gina thought, here she was just a human, not Tokari, not Raninali, not a half-blood. The questions she would be asked would be about her entire species and not about the individual choices her parents happened to make that resulted in the birth of this child that didn't fit in anywhere.

The locals walked on, leaving her at the station.

"Well, I guess it's time to get going," Gina said to herself. She picked up her bags and followed the basic directions that she'd gotten from her company.

3

Redall, Hunter

When Hunter arrived in Redall, he walked around the city to get his bearings. He was surprised to see only locals in a city of this size. He had expected a mix of breesians and other nationalities as well, like in his hometown Grantan. He went into a bar to have a drink and ask around about what to do next. He sat down and asked the bartender for a beer.

The bartender looked him up and down and said, “You don’t look or sound like you’re Liunian,” while handing over the drink.

"I'm not, I'm Tokari, is that a problem?" Hunter said, and he saw the bartender arch an eyebrow. He wondered if his Raninali heritage might mean something different in Redall.

“Not for me, it isn't, as long as you're paying for your drinks. But since you're new to town, let me warn you: stay away from the Raven District.”

“The Raven District?”

“Yeah, that’s a rough part of the city, only drug addicts, foreigners and breesians end up there. It’s only gotten worse the past few years, it’s best if you don’t go there.”

“Alright, I’ll keep it in mind, what do I owe you for the drink?” Hunter paid and left the bar to find a place to sleep.

One backpack and a Sanalia blade were all Hunter had on him. With such an elite Veronn clan weapon, Hunter stood out as someone not cross.

Hunter looked all over the city, but the hotels were too expensive. The bartender's advice had only made him more curious, so he headed to the Raven District. It was dark, but seemed peaceful and quiet, he had no idea what the warning was about.

As he walked through the district, he came across some neighbourhoods that seemed entirely breesian. Once he got into the heart of the district however, he started noticing shadowy figures, lurking in alleyways, exchanging hushed conversations.

A man bumped into him, "Excuse me," he said, and kept walking. A moment later, Hunter noticed his wallet was gone. The thief started running. Hunter chased after him into an alley.

Out of nowhere, the man was attacked by a shadowy creature. Hunter watched as the creature made swift work of his prey. After the creature left, he found his wallet in the bloodstains of what used to be the thief. He decided to hunt the creature down. The creature went into an old house at the end of the alley

Hunter silently opened the door; the house was dark. He stepped into the house and closed the door behind him. The house felt cold, old, and empty. It felt as if nobody had entered the house in years. He could see dried blood stains on the carpet, but it didn't stop him from exploring, he checked the ground floor and didn't find much. All he found was that whoever had lived here was likely a psychopath or a monster. Hunter went upstairs to check the next floor.

When he got to the next floor, there was a long hallway line with some pictures. He looked at the picture of a young girl and boy next to each other.

Suddenly, Hunter heard something fall; he looked around and saw a shadow of a person at the end of the hallway. The shadow started walking slowly towards him. Hunter felt the bloodlust coming from the monster. The light of the moon shone through the window on the monster. Hunter was now able to see it. The monster had long black hair, a human body, but claws so sharp it could easily slice down a tree and it also had a strong, earthy stench. Hunter unsheathed his blade.

"This just got exciting," Hunter grinned.

4

Kanera, Gina

A year ago, 6102

In her last year of university, Gina had heard about a new programme, the Djanian Outreach Project by Denma Corp.

Denma was one of the largest human corporations and had outposts in all human nations, they specialised in services like accounting, research, and human resources. They had begun pursuing government contracts. Several decades ago, they had expanded into Djania and had a significant outpost in the Djanian capital, Prancinia. The Outreach Project was the biggest contract a human company had ever gotten in Djania. It had surpassed the deal done 15 years ago by manufacturing giant Sunnico to develop a tech hub just outside of Prancinia. If Gina had not been accepted into the Denma programme, Sunnico would have been her next choice, hoping to get a job that would bring her to Djania. She, along with thousands of young graduates across Nüland, had applied to be a Djanian Outreach Coordinator. There were only 250 spots to be filled in the first, pilot edition of the programme.

Gina had sailed through the first two rounds of interviews. She'd assumed the third would be the same. When she'd entered the meeting room, she saw the first two interviewers that she'd met in the previous interviews respectively, but they were joined by a third. Gina managed not to gasp but she couldn't help staring. The final interviewer looked to be elven. Or wait, maybe he was human, she couldn't tell.

Most people her age didn't know about elves anymore; they were just another of the demons that had stayed on Thaedim after the two-hundred-year war ended. In her history classes at school, the textbooks had lumped all inhabitants of Thaedim under the category of demon. The only reason Gina knew the different species on Thaedim was because of Hunter: his clan history books had told a different story. His grandpa had been constantly grilling him on what kind of creatures he could encounter there. Though, in the books that Hunter had used, elves always had a murderous look on their faces, and not the slightly bored expression of the man in front of her.

Gina wasn't sure because he had sharply defined features and slight build, but he could just be a devastatingly good-looking human who was in the highest ranks of Denma while also being her age. No, definitely an elf.

The man caught her eye and pushed his hair behind his ear on one side. Sure enough, it was pointed. And most of all he'd seen her staring, blushing Gina quickly took her seat. Her mind was a half a world away from the interview. Thaedim's inhabitants were banned from leaving their island. If any demon came onto Nüland or Breeland, the Treaty would be void. So how could there be an elf here interviewing her?

Montel was amused, this was probably the first interviewee that had clocked what he was. The rest had mostly swooned a little, both men and women. He'd gotten bored of the reaction of unknowing humans decades ago. One who knew what he was… was interesting,

Montel was half listening to Gina's greetings with the other interviewers. She was following up on small details from her previous interviews in a way that Montel could see was swaying the interviewers in her favour.

He cleared his throat.

The two lower-level Denma employees jumped to attention.

"Let's begin." Montel said. He looked down at his paperwork, "Gina Hertfell, is it? You're from Grantan?"

Gina nodded, leaving it at that, and was pleased that she wasn't asked further about her heritage. "I was born and grew up there. I went to university here in Kanera, the Djanian studies degree."

"Have you been to Djania before?"

"Not yet. It's a dream of mine." With the other two interviewers, her earnest interest had helped her in the interview.

"Why is that?" Montel asked neutrally.

"Their tech, sir. And their culture, it's so much more advanced than ours." Gina stopped herself from talking about the accessories, surely that would make her look less serious as a candidate if she confessed that she loved the belts, bags, and necklaces, Djanian specialties. She'd managed to find some authentic pieces in Kanera, but most were copies. She couldn't wait to see the shopping streets in the capital, Prancinia.

Montel realised he hadn't introduced himself. "I'm Montel, I'm in charge at Denma for all Djanian projects. This is my programme."

Gina sat up a little straighter. Montel's eyes flicked to Gina's wrist where he caught a glimpse of something. "Tell me about your bracelet."

Gina moved to cover her wrist with her hand, too late. "Um this? I-I think it's a traditional Djanian design, I found it at the Djanian market in Grantan. There is this stall that is completely chaotic, but if you take time and really dig, you can find real gems." Gina blushed again, "well gems for me, that is, I found this woven and beaded necklace, and the breesian stall owner tied it into a bracelet. I've only seen a handful of them, but it reminds me of the Djanian carpets and textiles, with their impressive mix of colour and texture." Gina had written her thesis on Djanian textiles and how they complimented the innovation on the tech side with equally vivid textile art.

"I think you'll find that the necklace is from Rominore." Montel said mildly.

"Rominore? What do you mean?" Despite four years of her undergraduate degree, she'd never heard of anything out of Breeland that wasn't Djanian, even though there had been cursory introductions of the less well-known breesian nations of Rominore and Knett.

Montel chuckled, "I'm sure you'll discover more about it someday. Now," he said, turning to the routine questions in front of him, "How would you describe your approach to new cultures?"

Gina, a little wrong-footed, tried to shrug off the interaction and take the standard questions that she knew she could answer.

Three months later the letters announcing the successful candidates had been sent. She had been invited to Denma's Kanera headquarters for a two-week intensive training on Djania and her role in the new project.

5

Redall, Lnore

Thirty one years ago, the year 6072

Lnore was ten years old and sitting outside of her house in the breesian quarter of Redall. She'd arrived just six months ago. Her parents had worked hard to smuggle her out of Rominore. Lnore was pretending to be the niece of a kindly childless breesian couple, who had promised her parents that they would look after her.

Nülandish was difficult to understand, but speaking halting Nülandish was better than speaking her dialect to fellow breesians in the local community: her accent would immediately identify her Rominore origins, and she'd been warned about what would happen if she was identified as such in an otherwise almost entirely Djanian community. She knew there were others from Rominore and possibly Knett too, but there was no way to connect with them safely. And most of all, breesians needed a united front when so outnumbered by humans and living within human laws. She knew what would happen if she stood out.

She'd be sent back.

Sent back to the factories where the textiles were woven. Luxurious carpets and tapestries that would cover the floors and walls of Djanian dwellings. Djania was the only breesian nation to have formal relations with Nüland and so most humans thought that all breesians to be Djanians. Djania's rapid technological development put them far ahead of other breesian nations. The countries of Rominore and Knett had turned into a constant feeding system to satiate the Djanian need for raw materials. When there were occasionally products that required skill and finesse that the Djanians valued, other breesian nations shifted to serve that need.

Rominore had developed skills with textiles to feed Djanian investment. Their carpets and tapestries were more like works of art, and they became Rominore's main exports to Djania. They had reached a modest level of development thanks to the trade of textiles, and more recently, woven jewellery for tech with the Djanians. But they still needed workers, workers that could go blind from the close needlework. Workers that lost limbs in the massive looms. Workers that were scarred by the scalding dyes or choked on the toxic fumes.

Rominore workers could not afford gauntlets appropriate to the work that they were doing. Basic safety gauntlets could be rented from the factory, albeit at a cost that would continue the poverty cycle. Families would share gauntlets as well. Accidents were a daily occurrence. Lnore's mother had gone blind shortly after Lnore's birth. Her father's hands had been all but useless for being twisted into gauntlets that weren't designed properly.

Lnore's three siblings had all been picked off from her maimed parents to work in the factories. They'd managed to hide Lnore. When she reached the age that breesian children no longer immediately needed their parents, they had gone on a family trip to Nüland.

They had lived there together for a few months, the entrance visa allowing them some leeway and they moved further inland until they found the breesian settlement in Redall. They'd hope to blend in and that humans couldn't tell one breesian from another. Liunia, the country that they had arrived in, was unwelcoming to anyone different, human or breesian.

But Redall was a border city, so intermingling of different people had always been going on.

That only lasted a little while. Eventually, the authorities found her parents. Lnore had managed to remain thanks to the local couple. They had hidden her from the authorities and agreed to take her in.

But now here she was. Afraid to speak her own dialect outside the house and unable yet to speak the Nülandish that she heard around her.

"What are you staring at?" A breesian boy asked, his grey fur, fading to white on his legs, was distinctive.

Most breesians had fur ranging from golden to brown and sometimes red. Lnore was quite pleased with her golden fur that deepened to brown around her shoulders, she'd already had ideas of how she'd like to accentuate her colouring with stylish clothes and accessories, if ever she could afford such luxuries.

"Nothing." She replied in accented Djanian. The boy looked to be the same age as her and didn't seem to be a threat.

"Why haven't I seen you at school? You look like you should be in my class."

Not sure how to answer or if an answer was even necessary, Lnore shrugged.

This was how Brtann first met Lnore.

They spent the next 15 years, from childhood to adulthood, inseparable. Lnore eventually told Brtann about her nationality and illegal status in the human continent, but, once she learned he came from a Djanian family, she could not share her family's history.

She'd been conflicted that her best friend and the one person that had changed her life for the better, teaching her the Djanian accent, helping her learn Nülandish was from the same nation that had maimed her parents and separated her from them.

But Brtann had been born in Redall, she reasoned with herself. He didn't know what was going on. He must be innocent of what was happening on Breeland, right?

6

Ypare, Gina

A short walk from the train station, Gina found herself in front of the town hall. It was not the glossy organic architecture that the Djanians were famous for in their cities. It looked boxy, even industrial, despite the rural location. It seemed built for another, more prosperous time, when there were more citizens to serve. She could see that much of the lights were not in use and that it seemed that the top floors of the 4-story building were empty.

The automatic doors slid open as she approached. She walked in.

A Djanian reclined just inside the door. Breesians did not use desks and chairs, as such furniture was not suited to their anatomy. Their strong, thick legs and tail meant that balancing in a crouching position was the most comfortable way to get office work done. When not working, they tended to use couches to recline and fully extend their bodies. Gina had practised both the crouch and the reclining positions and found it very awkward. But she knew that the locals, especially when they haven't encountered humans before, would appreciate the effort, even if she could only sustain it for a short time.

She took a deep breath and said in Djanian, “Someone enters.” This was the common Djanian phrase for politely announcing yourself. She was a little embarrassed to hear her pronunciation and waited for a reaction.

The Djanian replied, "Someone is welcome." Although this could sound like a positive start to the conversation, Gina knew that they were still going through the formalities, and it would be some time before they reached anything of substance.

"This one is Gina." As she said this, Gina attempted to twitch her ears as a Djanian might on first introduction.

"This one is Rngal." The Djanian's ears turned towards Gina.

"This one is delighted to arrive."

"This one is delighted to see you safely here."

They continued with the formal greetings until Rngal stood up from the couch to stand in front of Gina. This was the indication that they could begin the substance of their conversation.

Gina's Djanian did not go much further, and she stuttered a bit as she mixed her Djanian and Nülandish together, "This one - uh - I have arrived from Denma Corp. I have been told to report to ada-Brtann."

In her own surprisingly clear Nülandish, Rngal replied, "Yes, I will bring you to him."

With a flick of her tail, Rngal indicated that Gina should follow.

Walking through the building that had been fully designed for Djanians, Gina tried not to stare too much at the rich textiles and tapestries that decorated the walls.

They stood before an office door, rather than knocking, Rngal opened the palm of her gauntleted hand and tapped gently on the door. A low acknowledgment of the tap could be heard. Rngal slid the door to the side and gestured for Gina to enter.

7

Redall, Hunter

Hunter stood before the creature, as it lunged forward with lightning speed, Hunter's reflexes were quicker. He effortlessly sliced the monster's head off in one smooth strike. The monster's body fell to the ground. Hunter put his Sanalia blade back in its sheath. He looked at the monster. The monster seemed to have once been human, but its hands were deformed. Its fingers had twisted and mutated into three vicious claws. Its mind was clearly gone as well. Hunter wondered what could do that to a human. But he was suddenly hit with a wave of the drugs that were in its system. He had to get away from the distinctive, earthy smell that was threatening to take over his senses. Dizzily, he stumbled away

He looked around the house, and he decided that he would try to find a place to collapse, since he was on the verge of passing out. On the top floor of the house there weren't any blood stains, and there was a room with one bed; it was a bit dusty, but clean enough. Hunter put his stuff down and slept.

The next morning, Hunter left the house and decided to look around the Raven District. It seemed suspicious that there were monsters here, he wanted to investigate. He looked around but couldn't find anything, he went back to the bar from the night before.

The bartender saw him, "What would you like to drink?"

"Same as last time," said Hunter.

"What do you think of Redall?" said the bartender

"It's a very interesting city, especially the Raven District," said Hunter.

"What do you mean? Don't tell me you went there after I told you that you shouldn't. You could have gotten yourself killed!" said the bartender.

"Yeah, I know now. Last night I ran into some kind of beast in the Raven District."

The bartender nodded, "Sounds about right. Say, what's your name."

"Hunter. Yours?"

"I'm Diego. Hunter, let me tell you what's going on in the Raven District. Ten years ago, it was a nice place with all kinds of people, but then about five-six years ago things changed. Casinos opened up everywhere and it became a place where people would gamble and get drunk and broke. The next thing we knew, half the residents were drug addicts, and some of those drug addicts have bizarre mutations, they lose their minds. Sounds like that's what you saw last night. Some people are beginning to say that it might have something to do with Sunnico, the big pharmaceutical company around here."

"Sunnico?" repeated Hunter, it was pulling at a memory that was just out of reach. After a moment, he added. "That sounds pretty bad."

After talking to Diego, Hunter left the bar. He thought to himself that he should help the people here, but even with combat training, he couldn't solve the problems of a whole city.

8

Redall, Brtann

Thirteen years ago, the year 6090,

Lnore had not been enrolled in school when they first met as children. Brtann had brought her into class with him one day, immigrants from Breeland were not uncommon and a handful of children were folded into the school system without question every year; it helped to hide them from the human authorities.

Brtann's motivation had been selfish: he'd wanted a friend in class. But it turned out that Lnore had a brilliant mind. She was constantly a step ahead of the teachers, making connections that they had not seen. She had achieved the highest levels of education and showed strong aptitude in engineering. Brtann's academic talents were nowhere near as impressive.

Breesians had their own school system that accommodated the relatively longer adolescence of their species. They did not reach adulthood until around 30 human years. Many decades ago, there had been attempts to integrate human and breesian schools, but the difference in the maturity rate in each species meant that both groups were underserved. The eventual result was that universities were open to both humans and breesians that had completed the primary and secondary school in their respective systems.

It was Lnore's focus on continuing her interest in design and engineering that had led them to university. Brtann followed a less demanding area of study. But they'd remained constant companions. He'd supported Lnore through her exams, keeping her fed and her morale up. He was also an excellent sounding board as she worried her way through some of the assignments. Since his classes were not terribly challenging, he had time to devote to Lnore, ensuring she achieved everything she could.

At the end of the last exams, Lnore and Brtann sat on the rooftop of their student dorm. Brtann sat close to Lnore but was careful not to get too close.

The genuine friendship that had sustained both of them through school had shifted for Brtann, as he'd watched Lnore finally come out of her shell and be able to use her brilliant mind for analysis and innovation. The work she had taken on as part of her degree had allowed her to shed a layer of guarded sadness that had kept her aloof from others, including him, for all those years before. He'd felt her finally opening up to him.

And he'd liked it; in fact, he loved it and loved her devotedly.

But he feared the walls coming back up if he confessed his feelings at the wrong time. He wanted her to take the lead if there was ever to be anything more between them.

"We did it," Lnore murmured happily.

"Well, I'm sure *you* did..." Brtann said.

"Don't say that! You'll be fine too, I know it." Lnore swatted at him playfully with her tail and then gingerly leaned into him. Brtann stayed very still. It was a start.

It took still some months before Lnore finally shared her feelings with him. Brtann immediately reciprocated. No one that knew them was surprised. Over the preceding months, they'd had this unconscious tendency to gently lean against each other and finish each other's sentences. The affection was clear.

It was not always the norm for breesians to choose life partners, but Brtann and Lnore had committed to each other. They lived in a human city and thus followed human norms when it came to pairing off.

When they married according to the human traditions, Lnore gained legal residency in Redall.

9

Ypare, Gina

Gina stepped into Brtann's office, stumbling a little on the thick rug. Djanian feet had thick, leathery pads that did not always require footwear. In cities, shoes were common, due to the hazards that may be on the ground, but it seemed, in this town, there was little trash, litter or sharp objects that would require shoes on any other than formal occasions. As a result, the floors had carpets of varying thickness, depending on the preference of the inhabitant.

Gina found her bearings and walked in the room. Brtann did not rise from his couch but was sitting in an upright position. His grey fur was uncommon for his kind, Gina had only seen one other grey-furred breesian, and that had only been since being in Djania. Brtann's accessories included leather layered necklaces with matching crossbody bag, one necklace in particular was more intricately woven than the rest. It was not unlike the bracelet that had caught Montel's eye during her interview process. His seeming careless overlapping of styles, though understated, brought to mind a slightly dated trend. Or perhaps a trend waiting to happen, Gina reflected.

With a flick of his tail, he indicated a chair that seemed to have been expressly brought in for Gina's human form. Internally she winced, she didn't want them to feel that she always needed this special accommodation, but she sat in the chair.

Rngal remained outside and, when she saw Gina settled, slid the door closed.

"So, you're Gina." Brtann said in perfect, Nülandish. Gina tried to place the accent, it sounded like the accent from Liunia, Gina speculated. The Djanians that Gina had known in her home country, had similarly flawless Nülandish, but that could only be developed after many years of immersion and study and often only to those breesians that had been born in human cities

She was also startled to hear him going straight into a conversation. She'd expected another round of formalities. A little off-balance she said, "Yes, Denma Corp has selected me to be the cultural interlocutor for Ypare, to help this town develop its knowledge of and interaction with humans. It's very nice to finally be here and I look forward to working together, ada-Brtann."

She saw Brtann's ears flick back, a sign of mild annoyance. Had she said something wrong?

"I prefer not to use the honorifics."

"Ah, I'm sorry, I didn't mean to offend," stammered Gina, not sure what to do. Her training was deserting her.

"Not a problem." The ears returned to neutral.

"I - I'm looking forward to learning about this assignment." Gina offered, trying to bring the conversation back on track.

Brtann blinked slowly, an indication that he'd accepted her attempt to restore the good feeling in the conversation. "It makes me glad to hear it. You will have two important roles. One will be here in the town hall, engaging with our staff. The other will be community outreach. We are interested in getting the young ones used to humans and see if they may be able to pick up human speech more easily if they hear it early enough."

Gina reeled a bit, all her interactions with breesians so far had led her to believe that they took time to impart messages and often left one message to be absorbed before introducing a new idea. Brtann was defying her expectations.

But she didn't mind, it might be good to have a confidant here, one that understood the chaotic flow of human communication.

"This is exciting and I'm very glad to join you." She blurted out - this was exactly what she'd always wanted - through years of study and her degree, she'd finally found her place: the bridge between humans and breesians.

10

Redall, Brtann

Ten years ago, the year 6093

Together, Lnore and Brtann moved out of the breesian quarter in Redall. They moved to the Raven District, a trendy neighbourhood that accepted different human nationalities and also different species, including breesians.

Lnore and Brtann had found a small flat above a shop with a workshop in the back. They didn't have much, but what they did have they poured into the small building.

Their idea had been to import small gadgets from Djania and sell them. There were numerous shops for everyday goods that fellow breesians would appreciate. But Brtann wanted to test an idea: he'd noticed that humans were increasingly curious about Djanian tech, and he wanted to create a store where humans could get a taste of the tech from his country, so much further ahead of the humans.

Lnore, despite her distaste for Djania, was fascinated by everything that Brtann brought back on his visits there. He invited her time and again to go with him, but she always declined, she'd promised herself that she would not step foot in the country that had ripped her family from her.

“You're sure you don't want to join me? You'd get to choose from the best, and not get stuck with whatever shiny gadget happens to catch my eye.”

“You have a surprisingly good eye,” Lnore said. It was true that Brtann had an excellent sense of what would sell. That's why they hadn't yet found an associate who could do the job for Brtann, which had been the plan in the beginning. “And besides, the only specific items are the tools we discussed last week. I'm fine here. I'm so close with the gauntlets...”

Brtann nuzzled her affectionately, he adored her ability to focus on a problem and not let go until she'd solved it or had definitively decided that it could not be solved. She'd been working on the gauntlets for months. Before that, he'd known that this idea had been bouncing around in her head since childhood.

Lnore's goal was to make a definitive pair of gauntlets for every task. They would end the need for different gauntlets depending on the nature of the activity. If she could make this work, they would have a game-changer. Her goal was to equalise the hierarchy among breesians. Wealth often dictated what a breesian could do in life, because nearly every job or activity required gauntlets. Poor families, like hers in Rominore, had only one pair of gauntlets that would allow her parents to work. Lnore had used a ragged pair of gauntlets borrowed from the school when she had begun attending in Redall, but they were clumsy and didn't function well. It limited her ability to complete schoolwork when motor skills were involved.

Brtann's family had been better off, they'd always been able to supply him with what he needed. At school, a place where he'd never thrived, he'd swapped his gauntlets for the Lnore's shoddy school pair. It had changed everything for her. Suddenly, everything fell into place.

Lnore wanted her gauntlets to be affordable, comfortable, and created on a mass scale. Most of all, they would give opportunities to breesians all over the world.

When they had first opened the store, Brtann had been chagrined when Lnore had taken apart many of the products he'd brought from Djania, seeing how they worked and often leaving it in pieces on her worktable, when it was meant to be in the shop. But he'd soon realised that once she figured it out, she could restore it to its original function and occasionally added an improvement or two.

11

Kanera, Gina

Six months ago, 6102

In the training that all new Djanian Outreach recruits had to take, Gina had sat through long lessons about Djanian culture, and she was bored, it seemed that not every recruit had her educational background.

At university, she had studied about how Djania had developed their technology without relying on magic. It had led the Djanians to develop much more quickly than Rominore or Knett. In her studies, not much was written about the interactions between Djania and its fellow breesian nations. Many of the courses and textbooks had been written in collaboration with Djanian scholars and took a very one-sided view on the history of Breeland and the current relationships between Djania and the other breesian nations. The human professors had little experience with Breeland and thus depended on the Djanian input with no way of verifying its accuracy. The war with Thaedim had accelerated Djanian innovation. Djanian soldiers, warships and eventually airships had blocked the demons from landing on the coast of the entire Breeland continent many times in the war.

In one of the training sessions, Montel showed up, he was going to lead the lesson. There was a palpable shiver that went through the room as all of the recruits noticed how good-looking he was. He ignored it and began his lecture on the *phana*.

"Although the demons of Thaedim relied on magic for their development and wartime weapon of choice, Djania had turned away from magic long ago as unpredictable and unreliable. I'm sure those of you here that have studied Djanian history will be aware of this." A few heads in the audience nodded, Gina's was one of them.

"Here on Nüland, we eventually also came to the same conclusion, well" he paused, "except for the warrior clans," he said dismissively.

Gina nodded again, this time because a small piece of the Montel puzzle seemed to have been inadvertently revealed. He was Nülandish, could he be half-elf, half-human? She didn't know if that was possible, but he did seem more human than the elves in the books, his ears, covered today by his hair, were only gently pointed, not the sharp, protruding features that were so distinctive for elves. He seemed to have a slight Eastern accent, but it was faint. Could he be from Emaich? He was continuing the lecture. She focused her attention on what he was saying.

"...since talent often skips generations and this results in an unreliable state of development. Djania was the earliest nation that turned towards technological development. This choice to eschew magic allowed them to outpace every other nation on their continent and the world. Their consistent progress over time allowed them to develop far beyond other nations that suffered from the fits and starts from magic-backed gigantic leaps forward, which could only be sustained as long as the powerful magic user was alive. Djanians did not allow their citizens that showed such magic-related talents to have families. If they wanted children, they had to renounce citizenship and move away. In a few generations, magic had been eradicated from Djanian society."

He paused again, a smile appeared on his face, devastating half the room. "But -and here's where it gets interesting- there *is* magic in Djania, an ancient spell, called the phana."

Gina's jaw dropped: magic in Djania? She leaned forward.

"I see that I've finally gotten your attention."

It felt like he was talking directly to Gina.

"Before the nations on Breeland had been created, just as the earliest breesian communities were being formed, magic was rampant on their continent. For early breesian communities, the family unit was the core basis of society. Separation from family members was unthinkable and the early breesian communities used an old and wild magic that was bonded to every breesian, and created the phana. This magic created an unbreakable bond that the land itself would defend and result in the death of whoever tried to break it. In the early years, it had mostly been used by families, but eventually friends and especially comrades in arms used the phana to remain together in case of capture. It is not used very much anymore. Djanians try to ignore its existence, but they are obliged to respect it."

A hand shot up in the auditorium, Montel nodded, and a young woman asked with emphasis, "Is it a *romantic* bond?"

"No." replied Montel flatly, shutting her down. He glared for a moment around the auditorium, making it clear that there was to be no more of that line of questioning.

He continued, "There have been studies done on the phana and it seems that it creates a telepathic bond between the breesians. Although they could not, ethically, study what happens if the pair are separated. Some limited experimentation showed that when it was a person tried to separate a phana-bonded pair, they seemed to suffer from difficulty in breathing. The conclusions from that study were that it could lead to death by asphyxiation of the threatening party. I understand that some investigations were done on geographical separation, and earthquakes were recorded if the pair was separated. It is very powerful, and unlike many types of magic, constant and unwavering." Montel's fascination with the phana came from his fractured family; if elves and humans had access to this kind of magic, his family might still be together.

Gina's hand shot up before she knew it. Montel nodded, his face slightly weary, he recognized Gina, and wondered what it could be. Hopefully not a repeat of the previous question. "How do they invoke the phana?" She asked, absorbed in the lecture.

"The phana is invoked at any time by reciting an ancient phrase and it must be accepted by the other person."

Gina kept her hand up, "What is the phrase?"

"That's not for this lesson, and besides, none of us are breesians, it won't work for us. Anything else, Gina, was it?"

"No." Gina said as her nose fell to her notebook, writing furiously on the paper in front of her.

Montel looked around again, there didn't seem to be any other questions, so he continued, "It is not invoked lightly and is rarely used in the modern era. Be aware that Djanians, who had attempted to eradicate all forms of magic in their society, are very sensitive around the subject of the phana. Denma needs our staff to know and be sufficiently respectful and discreet about this phenomenon, should it come up in your time there. Some of you will be going to very rural villages and there may be different reactions there."

He moved on to a few other topics, when they reached the end of his session, Gina saw her opportunity. Montel made a swift exit, walking quickly. She had to run to catch up.

"Um Montel? Sorry, could I ask you something?"

He turned reluctantly, "Gina," His eyes flicked to her wrist, where she still wore the Rominore bracelet. "Yes, go ahead."

"Where can I find out more about the phana? Are there books I can read?"

He arched an eyebrow, considering her request. He made a decision, "Yes, if you're interested, I can share with you some resources. Follow me."

He brought her through the Denma buildings, walking confidently. Gina jogged to keep up with him. She saw how the other Denma employees seemed to vanish out of his way. When they got to his office, she saw the nameplate next to his door: Montel Wanyd, Vice-President, Djanian Division.

"Wanyd…" Gina read, frowning, "like the clan from Emaich?"

Montel looked at her darkly and didn't answer. A cloud seemed to come over him. He thundered into his office and pulled a thick book from his bookshelf.

"Here." He said stiffly, "I want it back before the end of the training, you can leave it with my assistant before you go."

It meant that she had a little over a week. She clutched the book and backed out of his office. "Y-yes of course, thank you!"

Later that evening, she finally had a moment to herself to begin reading the book. She looked at the cover, 'Breeland and the Phana: a comprehensive guide,' and then gasped when she saw the author, Montel Wanyd.

Over the next week, she read every detail about the phana, she learned the invocation and discovered that there were ways to temporarily separate a phana-bonded pair, if the separation was of limited duration and both parties wanted it. She also learned that the only way to break the phana was for one of the pair to die.

12

Thaedim, Hunter

After a few more days in Redall, Hunter decided that he'd had enough of Nüland.

He had a detailed map of Thaedim; this map was one of the secrets of the warrior clans. It was one of the objectives of the illegal training expeditions should war ever break out again, the warrior clans would have multiple entry points onto the island. The Veronn clan was responsible for a specific route into Thaedim, via an unguarded stretch of beach, into the city Killgaris. Then through Dead-end Forest, to another city, Mendani, over the mountains to the Eternal Garden and back again. All the warrior clans followed different paths with the goal of reaching the Eternal Garden. If a clan member could get there, gather herbs from the garden and bring them back, they would be considered full warriors.

It was often the time when clan members discovered if they were Awakened or not. Back in the days of the war, most clan members were Awakened, but as peacetime continued, fewer, and fewer warriors could access the powerful elemental magic.

Hunter had trained his whole life for this final phase in Thaedim. Even if he felt ambivalent about doing it.

Hunter found his way to the coast and took a large part of his savings to buy a small motorboat. Days later, he arrived on Thaedim; he felt a change in the environment. He noticed that the atmosphere was different from the human continent. Hunter pulled his boat onto shore and hid it in a cave.

Hunter checked his map, noting that Killgaris was not far away.

Suddenly he was engulfed by flames. Through the fire, he could see that a dragon had stalked him on arrival. Thanks to his clan's Talent, the flames had no effect on him.

Hunter grinned, "hmm, I can finally test how strong I am, let's see if I can take this dragon down." Hunter took his blade from its sheath, took a deep breath and in less than a second he closed the gap to the dragon. As he was ready to slice the dragon's head off, the dragon was attacked from behind. Surprised, Hunter's attack faltered, and he drew back. The dragon flew away in pain. Hunter looked and saw in front of him a human. The man looked back at Hunter.

Another human on the Thaedim? This was interesting. Hunter looked at the man: his presence was strong; Hunter could tell that the man had experience in battle. Hunter's grip on his blade relaxed slightly as he studied the stranger, intrigued by the unexpected turn of events. The two made eye contact.

"Who are you?" Hunter asked, his voice steady, but tinged with a hint of caution.

The man replied, "Get lost, because of you I couldn't slay that dragon."

"What, for meat? Were you trying to eat a dragon?" Hunter asked, trying to lighten the mood.

"I haven't eaten for two days, I'm starving. I could have sold the dragon's skin in Killgaris. I'd have had money to eat for weeks, and I could've stayed in a guesthouse instead of on the street."

"Is it even possible to skin a dragon on your own?" Hunter asked, distracted. The man ignored his question and walked away, searching for food. "Why not go to Killgaris? You should be able to get some food there," Hunter yelled.

"I know, but I'm broke, so how am I supposed to eat if I can't pay for it?" said the man.

Hunter came up with an idea, "It just happens to be that I was on my way to Killgaris, if I pay for your food would you join me in my adventure?"

"Why do you want somebody like me to join you?"

"It's simple, we're two humans on Thaedim, it will be harder to attack us if we're travelling together. It's self-preservation, that's all. I'm heading to the Eternal Garden, you?"

The man stood silent for a few seconds, "Yeah, I'm heading there too. I'll join you, but you'd better treat me to some good food".

"Deal! I'm Hunter."

"Rowan," said the man, gruffly.

PART 2 - TRUST

Interlude 1

A ten-year-old Hunter lifted his wooden sword and pointed it at his grandpa.

"Are you ready?" he called.

Neil nodded, and Hunter charged forward. His grandpa parried the attack with his own wooden sword. Hunter's momentum made him careen off to the side, stumbling a little. But he pivoted quickly, regaining his footing.

"Good, strike again Hunter."

Hunter swung his sword once more, and, once again, he was rebuffed, this time with more force. Hunter bounced back, springing flexibly in response to his grandpa's attack. And then he did something that shocked his grandpa; he seemed to leave his defences down completely. Curious, Neil took the opening offered, and attacked with his sword. Hunter ducked under the attack with ferocious speed and angled his sword towards his grandpa's unguarded side. The sword hit nothing but air, Neil had only barely sidestepped in time.

"Very good Hunter, keep going."

And Hunter kept up the attack, until his grandpa was winded and had to stop. "That's enough for today. Good work."

Later that evening, Neil was sitting with his daughter. "He's getting faster. He can't seem to remember a single lesson I teach him in the classroom, but he memorises every fighting lesson like it's second nature."

"Well, we've been bred to be warriors, it *is* in his blood," she said.

"I didn't think that a half-blood would show such talent."

"Half-blood? Dad, really? Talik is from Raninale, he's not a different species from us. We've been over this." she said, not bothering to hide her annoyance.

Hunter's parents had married eleven years ago, and her family still didn't see Talik as one of them, even though he was the most accomplished goldsmith they had ever known, human or warrior. Hunter's mom was secretly convinced that her husband must have some magic skills to produce such magnificent creations.

And it had been her family that had hired him to work in the forges, while she had been away in Redall. The Veronn clan forges were famous throughout the continent of Nüland. Their craftsmanship was revered, even by Djanians. The clan's Talent to withstand burning heat, allowed them to forge the most refined and powerful swords. In the past hundred years of peace, the Veronn clan had maintained their wealth and status by the sale of high value, often decorative, weapons. They had hired Talik to cater to a high-end clientele, who were looking for personalised golden embellishments to their swords. Over time, the Veronn's realised that freeing Talik to innovate with his own designs on their swords resulted in true works of art that garnered even higher prices.

These days, very few people needed Veronn clan swords for their intended use.

13

Redall, Brtann

Five years ago, the year 6098

About three years after Brtann and Lnore opened their shop, it had become a success and a staple of the Raven District. Humans from different countries came to visit it. Brtann was especially well-known in the community for his distinctive colouring, but also turned out to be a great salesman. They fell into a comfortable routine with Brtann taking the sales floor and Lnore continuing her development of the gauntlets.

She had hit a wall in the development. Having been surrounded by humans for most of her life, she started thinking of their hands as a blueprint for her gauntlets' range of motion and capabilities. But she needed to study them more closely. Without access to a human for research purposes, she had grown frustrated. And so, for the last few months, she had been spending more time in the shop with Brtann. This support had freed him to look into advertising and marketing for their shop. Not that it needed much, word-of-mouth seemed to be doing its job for them, with a steady stream of customers into the shop.

One quiet evening, a human walked into the store just before closing. Brtann was alone, it was getting dark outside. The man swayed unsteadily on his feet and seemed to be trying to figure out where he was.

Brtann kept his distance. "Hello and welcome." He said evenly in hopes that this would not be confrontational. There had been some hostility in the very early days of the shop, but that was all over now.

The human said nothing but stared at Brtann.

He lunged violently to one side, his arms flailing, his hands looked to be midway into becoming claws, fingers seeming to grotesquely melt into each other. He crashed into expensive displays, knocking products to the floor. Next, he lunged in the opposite direction, still stumbling forward. He made groaning noises, but nothing that could be considered language.

The man was still moving forward, Brtann would be next if he didn't get out of the way.

In a swift movement Brtann slid behind the counter, he had a pair of gauntlets there, specifically for defence. He slid his hands into the gauntlets and faced the intruder.

He didn't want to harm the man.

He moved around behind the human who was still moving randomly. Brtann closed his arms around the man, lifting him off the ground. He carried the man to the door and pushed him out.

The man stumbled along the street incoherently. He did not seem to have noticed the redirection. He was still lashing out randomly at the air around him, most of the time colliding with nothing.

Brtann moved back into the store, locked it, and pulled the shutters down. He surveyed the damage as Lnore appeared from their flat. She saw the mess and rushed to Brtann to see if he was alright. Standing with Lnore, Brtann's adrenaline crashed. He began to tremble violently. The damage to the store was minimal, despite the mess, but his mind was wracked with what-ifs.

What if the man had gotten through to their flat?

What if he'd gotten to Lnore?

What if Brtann had been forced to attack?

What if the human was injured and came back with the authorities?

Despite his fear, he'd managed to de-escalate in a manner that should not have inflicted any harm on the human. Even if the Raven District encouraged intermixing of different species, the Redall authorities were very much on the human's side, if ever there was a dispute with a breesian.

His face dropped onto his wife's shoulder; his tail thudded to the floor as he leaned heavily against her. She urged him away from the shop and back to their flat.

14

Ypare, Gina

Brtann rolled off his couch and stood before Gina. His height was a little intimidating as Gina scrambled out of her chair to stand up. He towered over her.

"I guess it's time to show you your new home." He said.

He walked over to a panel on the wall that held different types of gauntlets. Gina thought the display was an elegant way to integrate beauty in the presentation of a daily necessity for breesians. Brtann selected a pair and fastened them onto his hands. He closed his gauntleted fists a few times and turned to the door. As he walked out, he flicked his tail to indicate they were leaving. Gina followed.

The gauntlets that Brtann had put on allowed him to carry both of Gina's suitcases with apparent ease. They also, oddly, looked a little like claws, if she thought about it. She tried not to.

She picked up her backpack and followed him, even though there were a few vehicles out front of the town hall, Brtann had decided they would walk. Twenty minutes later they arrived at a small building. The building manager met them. She looked cheerful. It appeared that she'd tried to research what humans found homely and had decided that an apron was the perfect accessory to welcome the new foreigner. Her ears twitched forward encouragingly.

“Someone is welcome.” She said in Djanian.

“Someone has a wonderful establishment.” Gina replied.

Her new landlady was excited to host this human that would be living in her building. Out of the corner of her eye Gina couldn’t help but think that Brtann had just twitched his tail in quiet amusement at the exchange.

They climbed two flights of stairs, adjusted to Djanian legs, which made it about three in Gina's estimation. The stairs were on the outside of the building, and each floor seemed to be its own dwelling.

As they reached Gina’s new home, the landlady slid the door open - door knobs were far too finicky for Djanian hands. She stepped back, “This one will leave you now,” she said.

As her landlady was retreating, Gina remembered her training. “This one thanks you,” she called after her. She was rewarded with a small, pleased swish of her new landlady's tail as she disappeared down the stairs.

“You’ve studied our greetings well.” He said in Nülandish.

Taking her opportunity Gina replied, “This one is ever so pleased to be here,” in Djanian.

Despite himself, Brtann offered the Djanian version of a chagrined smile: his tail thumped a few times on the floor.

15

Killgaris, Hunter

Hunter and Rowan walked to Killgaris. They stopped at the first restaurant they saw, sat down at a table, and ordered some food. After they ate, they started talking.

Hunter learned that Rowan had studied several martial arts and that he could break a brick wall with a single punch. He too had been training since he was a child.

"No way!" Hunter said, "You're from the Frithe clan? You're also here to complete your training? I should've guessed, especially if you can take down a dragon."

"You sure you're from the Veronn clan? I mean not everyone has a Sanalia blade, but maybe…" Rowan unwisely had tried to discover Hunter's origins. He'd never seen a Veronn clan member with such dark skin.

"Maybe, *what*?" Hunter asked with emphasis.

"Nothing!" Rowan backed off and returned to the conversation "I'm training to see if I might be Awakened. It's been several generations…"

Hunter let it slide. Instead, he said: "In the Veronn clan, too! we haven't had anyone Awakened since we ended the Thaedim War," Hunter interrupted.

"The Veronn clan ended the war? Yeah, that's what they *would* think," Rowan countered. "If it hadn't been for the Frithe, you would never have gotten far enough into Thaedim to set fire to those cities."

Hunter shrugged; he didn't care too much about the details of history. But Rowan seemed fired up. "It's bad enough that the regular humans look down on the Frithe, we don't need other warrior clans doing it too."

Hunter shrugged again and said, "I grew up in the clan system too, the rest of the kids looked down on all of us."

"In Liunia there's a lot less tolerance than in Tokarei. You've got anti-discrimination laws. In my country, it's not like that. If you're different, you have to fight, whether you're Djanian or from another country," Rowan looked pointedly at Hunter, "or clan kids like us. Luckily for the clans, fighting comes naturally."

"That's true," Hunter conceded. "My best friend is a normie. She learned a lot about the warrior ways because of how much time we spent together."

"I can't imagine that, whenever I was unlucky enough to cross paths with kids from mainstream schools, they would attack me, throwing rocks, mocking the Frithe clan's magic. I would love to be Awakened, just to show them what real power is."

"I'm not so sure." Hunter replied, "My grandpa seemed to think that magic *that* powerful only emerged when it was needed in the world, so maybe, if it's gone for good, that means we're living in more peaceful times?" Hunter said thoughtfully.

"I don't know about that. My brother, Dan, was murdered in Redall five years ago. Some drugged up creature attacked him out of nowhere, big, like a Djanian."

"Redall? I was just there. I can tell you it hasn't gotten better. I was also attacked by some drugged creature that looked half human half animal. In the Raven District."

"Sounds about right," Rowan said tightly. Hunter could see that Rowan was still furious about Dan's death.

"Well, if we get out of this year alive, how about we go back to the Raven District and find the creature that attacked your brother. After a year here, one druggie shouldn't be a problem."

Rowan shook himself, trying to clear his head, "Yeah, that sounds good. First order of business is getting to the Eternal Garden and back. Then we can deal with the rest."

Hunter was content that Rowan seemed like a trustworthy person. After talking for hours, they finally left the restaurant. They explored Killgaris and were disappointed with how calm the city was. This was Thaedim: shouldn't danger be lurking around every corner? The Raven District had been more threatening.

Rowan wanted to leave the city. Hunter recalled passing a store that would sell them supplies for the journey. They found some camping and food supplies for a few days, but Hunter's money was running out. They would need to find some gold soon to get through this trip. They set up camp on the outskirts of Killgaris.

Hunter searched his pack to see if some money might have gotten stuck in the bottom, when he came across the envelope his parents had given him. It looked full. For a moment he was thankful for the extra cash they had sent with him. He tugged the envelope open, hoping some bills would spill out. But he was disappointed, medical notes and blueprints fell out in front of him, in the top corner of a few pages he saw the Sunnico logo. "Sunnico? Again?"

He tried to make sense of a few pages, but gave up after a few minutes, shoved everything back in the envelope.

"What the hell mom?" He muttered to himself as he got ready to sleep.

16

Ypare, Brtann

Brtann, who had selected the flat for Gina, surveyed the accommodations that had been made to allow a human to live there comfortably. Chairs and a matching table that were suitable for a human had been found; adapters and converters had been arranged by Denma Corp. The kitchen and toilet had been a challenge, with everything being adapted to a species with entirely different nutritional and anatomical needs, but they'd managed to find suitable, if slightly crude adaptations.

Brtann had arranged for some human foods along with human utensils. These would be hard to get in Ypare and opportunities to visit the capital Prancinia were not going to be frequent. So, Gina needed everything to live comfortably for a few months at least.

The Djanians were world leaders when it came to plumbing and effective use of water resources. They valued cleanliness very highly and their infrastructure know-how was in high demand. Brtann felt that this was one area where, even in a Djanian small town, Gina's experience would be elevated, having himself spent many years in the relatively disappointing human-developed water infrastructure. Bathrooms were elaborate, luxurious affairs even in relatively simple flats like the one Brtann had foreseen for Gina.

The flat had two rooms: a living/dining/kitchen area and a sleeping room. The bathroom was about the same size as the sleeping area. Everything looked far too large for Gina. Brtann was pleased that he'd thought of a variety of stepping stools so she could reach the counters, sinks, and bathtub.

He realised he was still holding her suitcases. He gently set them down on the floor. The gauntlets not only made his grip stronger but absorbed the weight of whatever he carried. Brtann closed his fists to try to conceal the very obvious claws on the end of each finger.

"I hope you will be happy here. We tried to arrange for the essentials, but if there's anything you're missing, just let me know and I'll take care of it for you."

Gina had been roaming around the small flat opening cupboards and trying to see how her stuff might make this place home. She opened a few kitchen cabinets and noticed some rice and canned food she recognized. She'd been prepared to go native with the food, and suffer the well-known digestive consequences, but was happy to see that it would not be such an extreme shift from one day to the next.

"This all looks very good, thank you. I guess I will begin tomorrow, shall I go directly to the town hall again?" She asked, still preoccupied with exploring the flat.

"Yes, that works. We prefer to start early and end before sundown as the winter days get shorter, so if you can be there just after sunrise, that would be 7:30 as you know it, we can begin then."

Gina nodded and ended the conversation with the traditional greeting "This one will be pleased to be of use."

Brtann blinked slowly accepting her turn of phrase and for the first time spoke in Djanian to Gina: "This one looks forward to our continued cooperation." And stepped out the door, opening his fist to palm the door closed. He winced internally as the claws flashed again.

He covered the ground at his normal speed, without having to shorten his steps to accommodate Gina's gait. He made it back to the office in half the time.

He passed by Rngal; they didn't speak but he could tell that she was quietly excited about Gina's arrival. Brtann proceeded to his space. With the door closed he deactivated the gauntlets, with a flick of the wrist. They slid gently into the holders that were mounted on the wall. There were a variety of other types for different purposes, but he tended to always come back to these. They had been with him a long time and reminded him of another life, one that had been both more violent and more vivid.

He had accepted that this was all he could do now with his special skill set, even if it sometimes grew monotonous.

His in-depth knowledge of human cultures had qualified him for this government project that was aiming, with Denma Corp, to see what early exposure and integration of humans and breesians could bring to facilitate inter-species understanding.

Gina was a good find; she was eager and open minded. But did she have the endurance to go through months of repeating the same lessons, greetings and confronting the same stereotypes over and over? Even Brtann found it tedious.

Humans were impatient, it had offered them agility in development, but resulted in half-finished plans much of the time. Djanians were the most dedicated to investigation and research of all the breesian nations. It was what had fuelled their technological development, strategic achievement after achievement with very few missteps.

Brtann was inclined to trust that, this time as well, the strategy was sound.

17

Redall, Lnore

Five years ago, the year 6098

The morning after the random intruder invaded their shop, Brtann and Lnore cleaned the mess together and prepared to open for another day. They were certain of two things: they needed a human on their side; they needed gauntlets that would make any human stand down.

Brtann told Lnore how this attack was not the petty anti-breesian vandalism that they'd experienced in the first weeks after the shop's opening. That had consisted mostly of spray-painted slurs and rude teenagers.

This invasion had seemed randomly violent. They had heard of a handful of similar incidents in the Raven District but had considered it gossip that was trying to undermine their new home.

Brtann prepared an ad for a human shop assistant.

Lnore returned to work on her gauntlets.

Before long, Brtann hired Greg, a new, human sales assistant with a sunny disposition. Greg and Brtann worked well together. Greg was fascinated by Djania and had visited once a few years back. He was exactly the target market that Brtann had had in mind when they opened the shop.

Greg loved Djanian gauntlets, he had a small collection, even though there was no way he would ever be able to make them work for his human hands. He even decorated his flat with the gauntlets mounted on the walls, as was the custom in Djania. Since Djanians needed a variety of gauntlets for different tasks in the day, having them accessible via the specialised wall mounts meant that they could easily change gauntlets as they moved from task to task. Greg's collection included gauntlets for cooking, sports, battle, and art. Brtann wanted to bring Greg with him to Djania at some point, but they weren't profitable enough yet to make that possible.

At the same time, Lnore was working on the gauntlets. Although her modifications until this point had been useful for daily life, she now began to think about modifications that could protect the wearer from harm.

Lnore had never associated as much with humans as Brtann, she'd been wary of Greg at first. But over the last few months, they'd developed a tentative friendship. He was fascinated by the innovations that she'd been doing with the gauntlets. She was fascinated by his hands and took advantage of his presence to kick-start her work on the gauntlets. Close observation of Greg's dexterity could help refine her design to mimic the all-purpose nature of human hands.

On slow afternoons Greg could be found in Lnore's workshop picking items up, holding things, performing a variety of everyday tasks to help her refine the range of motion. Once she'd seen everything that human hands were capable of, she decided to expand the range of motion and secure the grip in her gauntlets.

As she perfected the motion and responsiveness, she'd had another idea, to have them absorb the weight of heavy objects. It had taken months to figure out, but once she had, Brtann could find his wife using her gauntlets to carry Greg around the room, each time he saw it, he chuckled.

There hadn't been a subsequent encounter like the one with the drugged human, but Lnore's blueprints already had incorporated the vicious claws that would make the wearer fully able to defend themselves. She hadn't yet made a prototype with the claws.

18

Ypare, Gina

On her first day of work, Gina arrived exactly at the hour agreed with Brtann. Denma had prescribed an approximate uniform for the humans in Djania: a button-down top with slacks. It offered little possibility for variety or individuality, but it was also guaranteed not to be a cultural misstep with the Djanians, who were known to be very fashionable in the big cities, with outlandish trends and abstract shapes in clothing and accessories. But the countryside was different, most of the town's residents favoured tunics of a variety of colours and styles with slacks, accented with necklaces and belts.

"Someone enters" Gina called as she stepped into the building. Today was different: it was a normal working day, and all the town hall staff were in place. There were 50-60 Djanians in the large open-plan office area that had been deserted the day before. Some were working, others talking. Some were drinking the gmatta tea that was the traditional morning beverage. Gina had enjoyed coffee at her flat first thing in the morning and had been practising with drinking gmatta but found its bitterness hard to stomach in the morning and did not want to seem childish by adding sugar to her tea.

But the tea was far from her mind as everyone in the room broke off their conversations and stared as she walked through the entryway and into the main shared working area. Gina looked for Rngal or Brtann, but neither of them seemed to be around. She tried something: "This one is new. And has come to work with all in this place."

A few Djanians' ears perked toward her encouragingly, but most went back to what they were doing. Finding one seemingly still interested, Gina approached deferentially, "This one is looking for ada-Brtann or ada-Rngal."

The Djanian, a male with glossy beige fur replied, "This one will take you to them." He led her through the same hallways as the day before and they arrived at Brtann's office door. Gina wondered if she could go directly here the next time but feared that etiquette required her to greet her colleagues on arrival. In the Denma Corp training, they had encouraged interactions with the local town hall employees, who - although they likely didn't see themselves that way- were, in fact, one of the targets of the programme and thus would also benefit from positive interactions with humans.

As they approached the door, they could hear low conversation between Brtann and Rngal. The new Djanian tapped on the door. Rngal appeared after a moment, sliding the door open.

"The pet is here," Gina's companion said to Rngal, turning away from her dismissively. Gina had understood what he'd said, and her eyes widened a bit at the insult. Rngal caught the reaction, but did not react to her colleague, who was already walking away.

When he was out of earshot, Rngal turned to Gina, indicating her to come in. She said in very precise Nülandish, "This is a new programme and not everyone in Ypare is supportive. But we have the backing of the central government, which all of them believe in. We won't change everyone's mind, but they should all respect the government's plan."

Brtann was crouched behind his low desk, in addition to his tablet, there were several piles of paperwork. He gestured for Gina to take a seat, Rngal went to a low couch.

In Nülandish, Brtann said: “Rngal is right. It's not helpful and not going to make things easier, but it's good that you've already seen it. There are residents here that feel our programme is an entirely unnecessary use of time and resources. And perhaps it's good to share,” Brtann's eyes and ears flicked to Rngal as if asking for permission, she blinked once to agree. “It's not just you that has been brought here for this programme. It is also Rngal and me. I arrived two years ago and began the effort to introduce human culture and society. I have shared stories and experiences with many of the townspeople. Rngal is from Ypare. She returned about a year ago, after living many years in Prancinia. She knows the community much better than I do and so, on your community outreach days, she will accompany you for the first few months. Until you get your footing. But all of this is to say that there are those that look at not just you but the three of us as a waste of time, resources, and effort. We will not convince everyone, but we may open some minds along the way.”

Gina nodded: “I mean I’m not that surprised actually. I’m sure you know that on Nüland, not every community has been welcoming to Djanians. In Tokarei we’ve worked towards equality between breesians and humans, even though it’s still not perfect, it's better than in Liunia, where there is still a long way to go.” As she said this, Brtann stiffened imperceptibly.

Rngal spoke up: “It is good that you have some understanding of these issues. They will happen again. Brtann or I will be there, should anything happen.”

At that moment, the Rominore bracelet that Gina always wore slid past the cuff of her blouse. It immediately caught the attention of both Rngal and Brtann.

“Where did you get that?” Rngal asked severely, indicating Gina’s wrist.

“A-at a Djanian market back home, but I’ve been told it’s actually from Rominore…” Gina ventured, remembering her interview.

"Exactly. In the interest of not further alienating the sceptics. I'd recommend that you don't wear that to work." Rngal said sharply.

"Surely Rngal, that's too much," Brtann protested mildly.

"I know the people here and I know how they will react if they think this is a political statement."

"A political statement? But how...?" Brtann asked.

"You newcomers!" Rngal snarled. "You come here, and you pretend to know what the situation is because you've seen more of the world than we have. But trust me on this one. We're too close to the border for this to be seen as anything other than a Free Rominore symbol."

"It's fine!" Gina said and started fumbling with the cords of the bracelet, tugging it off her wrist. She slid the bracelet into her pocket.

19

Prancinia, Danica

Five years ago, the year 6098

Danica stood in yet another tech bargain shop in Prancinia. Her goal was to have a mainstream manufacturing success for her company, Sunnico. Danica's Djanian language skills were limited so she always had a translator with her and, by this point, was accustomed to the slow progression with negotiations.

She knew that she should have her team do this job, but she liked combing the aisles of cluttered shops. Despite the talent she knew she'd hired, she still believed that she had the best eye for spotting potential winners.

Brtann was also on one of his periodic visits to Djania and found himself in the same shop, looking for new products. As was often the case now that the development had progressed, he had a prototype pair of Lnore's gauntlets on.

Danica had been digging fruitlessly through box after box of discarded or out-of-use kitchen gadgets, from blenders to cutlery. Danica was convinced she could find a Djanian tool that she could repurpose as a best seller for the human consumers. But today seemed to be a bust.

She didn't look up when Brtann settled in, digging into a bin in the opposite aisle. His objective had been the same, although his scale was drastically smaller.

When Danica glanced up, she saw his smooth movements and graceful manipulation of the items that he pulled out of the bin with ease. Nearly 20 years of travelling back and forth between Redall and Prancinia and she'd seen how essential gauntlets were to the Djanians and she'd seen them evolve over the years.

She'd never seen a pair like this.

Her brain started ticking, maybe she'd missed another market that was in plain sight: the Djanians. She meant all breesians, but her mind did not make that distinction.

Gauntlets were an everyday essential for Djanians, if she could manufacture a pair that could have the all-purpose effortless efficiency that she saw in front of her, they could move out of the gambling business and start to work on mainstream products as well.

She had to know if these gauntlets were already being sold somewhere and if she could meet with the company owner.

20

Dead-end Forest, Hunter

The next day, Hunter and Rowan entered Dead-end Forest. After walking for some time, it seemed as if they were being followed by someone, or rather something. The two stopped walking and checked their surroundings to see if someone was there, but neither could see anything.

"Did you feel that?" Rowan whispered, his eyes scanning the surroundings.

Hunter nodded, his senses on high alert. The feeling of being watched persisted, and the air seemed charged with an unsettling energy. The forest, despite its name, seemed to hold secrets that transcended the ordinary.

As they cautiously continued their journey, the creature that they could now sense behind them kept following. They could feel the creature's killing intent. Hunter instinctively reached for his Sanalia blade, and Rowan tightened his fists. Hunter took a knife from his side pocket and threw it into the trees. A body fell from the tree and hit the ground. Hunter walked to the body but stopped.

The body started moving and got up on its feet. "It's been a while since a human entered this forest" said the body while regenerating the part where Hunter's blade had hit him. The creature's body grew around the knife, engulfing it.

Hunter and Rowan looked at it.

“Who the hell are you?” yelled Rowan.

“I don't have a name, but I have been called the guardian of the forest”. His body grew bigger, and two more arms started growing out of it. “Yes, I am the Guardian of the Forest”.

Hunter took his blade out of its sheath. “I take it that we can’t walk through here without a fight.”

Hunter and Rowan got ready to fight. The Guardian chuckled, the sound echoing through the dense trees. The air became tense as the atmosphere crackled with an otherworldly energy. The Guardian's eyes glowed with an eerie light as he observed the two intruders.

“Indeed, humans. You cannot simply walk in this forest without facing the consequences,” the guardian proclaimed, his voice resonating with an ancient power.

Hunter tightened his grip on his sword, exchanging a quick glance with Rowan. The duo shared a silent understanding and prepared for the confrontation.

The Guardian lunged forward with astonishing speed, his multiple arms slashing through the air. Hunter skilfully parried the attacks with his sword, while Rowan landed a serious punch. The guardian flew back and hit a tree.

“I see, you two are different from the other humans that I have encountered. A Constant and -maybe- a Superior? Oh well, doesn’t matter. I’ll finish this quickly,” said the Guardian.

21

Prancinia, Brtann

Five years ago, the year 6098

"See that Djanian, I'd like to talk to him. Can you make the introduction?" Danica said softly. The translator was mortified, this was not how Djanians interacted. They waited for formal introductions; they did not bother other Djanians going about their business unless it was an emergency. The translator did not see the emergency, but she also knew it was not a question.

What only the translator noticed was the way Brtann's ears swivelled towards them when Danica spoke. She intuited also from his body language that he must have understood what Danica said.

The translator decided to play along with a show to Danica that she was willing to go above and beyond Djanian norms to facilitate her client's needs. Danica was oblivious.

The translator glided over to where Brtann was standing and stopped a respectful distance away. In Redall both breesians and humans would have just called across the aisle to speak with someone. But this was Prancinia, norms must be obeyed. Brtann, himself, having been born and raised in Redall, sometimes struggled to conform to the expectations in Djania, so he was a bit taken aback when the translator appeared not far away from him in the same aisle.

"This one hesitates to interrupt." The translator said softly, politely.

"This one finds no fault." His formal Djanian was not fluent, having mostly used the everyday language to speak with Djanians in Redall.

The translator processed this. Her fluency in all levels of Djanian made switching between levels of politeness second nature. But this situation was slightly different. "This one is accompanying an honoured guest." The translator's ears flicked to where Danica stood, still pretending to casually search a bin, with one eye on the conversation.

Brtann's nose flicked in Danica's direction, but he did not move otherwise. The translator's statement did not require more from him.

"The honoured guest is interested to know the one in front of me."

Brtann was suddenly amused. The translator was tying herself up in knots to try to adhere to the formal sequence of greetings and connect her human client to Brtann in some way. His tail thumped lightly on the floor.

The translator's mortification tripled. He was laughing at her. She started to spiral into her own pit of shame, her tail curled tightly beneath her, and her ears flattened in embarrassment. Brtann realised he needed to do something to restore the balance.

To Danica's eyes, the two had barely moved and there had been only a slight growling back and forth. She was trying to be patient, she'd learned that when dealing with Djanians, there were certain things that could not be rushed.

"This one is pleased to meet the honoured guest." Brtann replied quickly. The translator's body uncurled slightly, and she blinked in relief at Brtann. A flick of her tail indicated she should follow him. He hesitated, "is not this the honoured guest?" His ears flicked over the aisle.

"Y-yes." The translator looked confused.

Brtann felt guilty. When should he confess that he'd understood the translator's mission and was bilingual with Djanian and Nülandish? He did not like confessing his birth abroad when in Djania. He noticed that the natively born Djanians tended to look down on him. He'd developed a technique of approaching store staff with his casual Djanian as a tactic in negotiations. No one had yet realised that it was a cover for his imperfect polite Djanian.

But the translator had noticed. Language was her playground and her precision with it meant that she could detect any number of accents and imperfections without effort.

In a more casual Djanian Brtann, he said, "This one speaks Nülandish and understands the culture. This one will call over the aisle." And in a concession for the awkward job she'd been asked to do, he offered, "This one is Brtann."

Taken aback, she offered: "This one is Rngal of Ypare."

PART 3 - POWER

Interlude 2

When Tokarei had passed its anti-discrimination laws, there had been a wave of immigration, not the least from the southern desert country, Raninale. Gina's father, Menali, had been one such transplant. He was a scholar who had originally gravitated to Kanera to join their university as a lecturer but hadn't succeeded there. Eventually he found himself in Grantan, teaching at a non-descript high school.

So far to the north in Tokarei, there were few Raninali immigrants, so when Menali encountered Talik, they became friends more out of convenience than genuine shared interests.

From when Gina was about twelve, a few times a week, her dad would pick her up from school and together they would visit the Veronn clan forges. Talik's son Hunter was often around, so he and Gina ended up spending long hours together, while their dads caught up. To Gina, ten-year-old Hunter was just a kid and she felt that she was mostly being informally asked to take up babysitting duties while their dads caught up.

On yet another slow-moving afternoon, Hunter was complaining: "It's dumb, grandpa keeps making me read all these books about the warrior clans and Thaedim, but history is so boring. Why can't I spend all my time fighting? We're a *warrior* clan, aren't we? And I'm actually *good* at fighting."

Gina was thoughtful. "I like reading, can you show me some of those books? Maybe we can read them together, after all, our dads are gonna be talking for hours, it'll give us something to do."

Hunter rolled his eyes, "Why don't we fight? I could show you some new attacks I've been practising."

"No way! If that's what you want to do, I'll just work on my homework by myself."

For the next couple of weeks, they stayed in their separate corners, Gina doing schoolwork and Hunter practising his fighting moves. But eventually they got bored of their respective activities and decided to try again.

Hunter brought his Veronn clan history books. Gina's eyes lit up. A few weeks later, Gina was hooked. She rushed her dad every time they were meant to go to the forges.

"Look what it says here," Gina pointed to a paragraph in Hunter's book, "There used to be magic users and warriors that lived everywhere on Nüland. That's not what my textbooks say! They only talk about the established warrior clans in Somden, Tokarei, Liunia, and Emaich. But Raninale had magic users once too!"

"What does that matter?" Hunter asked.

"Well, it means that magic isn't contained to one location or one group of people. Raninale is looked down upon because they don't have a warrior clan, but if your history books are correct, they had magic users and warriors, but because they did not enter the Thaedim War, their warriors and magic users migrated to join the fighting. Do our dads know about this?"

Hunter was already only half-listening. "Maybe, I don't know. What else?"

"It says that the Strannae clan was the first to be established, in Somden. They wanted to use magic to find ways to heal the injured in the fighting, eventually developing the Talent of fast healing. Then Wanyd emerged from the ship-borne soldiers, who had to fight off the Thaedians at sea. They developed the Talent of breathing underwater. Then it was your clan, the Veronn, who forged weapons for the war in blazing forges. As you know, your Talent means you can't be burned. Lastly, the Frithe clan, always the brawlers among the warriors, they did not have a specific goal beyond defending Nüland from the invasion. Their Talent is durability."

"Strannae, Wanyd and Veronn found a place for their talents after the war, as healers, seafarers, and weapons makers even today. The Frithe clan, however, has fallen on hard times, because they never managed to find a new, unifying goal after the war ended. So that's why Liunia has become such a rough place to live, with discrimination and a lot of violence! That's not at all what they say at school!" Gina said, deeply absorbed.

Hunter looked at her "And so..."

"And so, Hunter, you have here a completely alternative history! Can I borrow this book?" She asked, indicating another thick book titled 'Demons of Thaedim: An Encyclopaedia'.

Hunter shrugged, "Sure."

She went home happily with the book tucked under her arm.

22

Ypare, Gina

For the rest of her first day at work, Gina filled out paperwork and then was paraded out to meet each of the colleagues at the town hall. The names swam in her mind, but when Gina finally again stood in front of the Djanian male from earlier that day, she remembered his name, Nkano. This time she was bracketed by Brtann and Rngal, but she could feel his dismissive attitude. The rest of the staff mostly seemed disinterested.

As they were ending the day, Gina dared to ask the question that had been on her mind all day: "Tomorrow morning, when I arrive, shall I go directly to your office? Or do I have a desk? Maybe one of you can be here to meet me?"

Brtann and Rngal's ears twitched towards each other. Brtann deferred to Rngal, he stepped back to indicate that she could use her expertise as it was something that they foolishly hadn't considered.

Rngal said, "Tomorrow we will begin with our first outreach in the town, I'll meet you at the building's entrance and we will go directly." Rngal turned to Brtann and spoke in slow, easy-to-understand Djanian, "Then perhaps someone might have time during the day to discover Gina's space in the town hall." She deliberately spoke slowly enough so that Gina could understand. Brtann's tail thumped once on the floor in agreement. For the most part, Gina's role was to be outside the town hall, visiting the community. They hadn't thought that she would be there long enough to require her own space in the town hall. But now it seemed essential.

"This one is very pleased with the plan." Gina smiled at Rngal.

The next morning, Rngal was at the entrance waiting for her, Gina called the traditional greeting as she entered. There was less reaction this time, though she could feel a few glances directed her way.

Rngal walked towards her immediately and they left the building together. Rngal had reserved a vehicle from the town hall fleet and drove Gina to their first appointment.

Djanian motor vehicles had made it to Nüland and were becomming common place. They allowed Djanians to travel distances with ease. It was Gina's first trip in one. The interiors were designed for breesian bodies, so Gina half-stood and hung on to the roof as Rngal crouched comfortably into the driver's seat. In Somden, they had developed a motor vehicle, but those were unreliable, expensive, and uncomfortable. They were still seen in Somden, but the rest of the continent had decided to import the superior Djanian vehicles, adapting the interiors to suit human bodies, allowing humans to sit in relative comfort as they drove around. The vehicles were still mostly used by the middle and upper classes.

"This morning was a lot better, thank you." Gina said as the vehicle passed through the small town centre.

"I'm sorry we weren't there yesterday. But once we've found you a suitable workspace, we can spend more time at the town hall, and you can meet the friendlier colleagues. They're not all like Nkano. Normally, I would have briefed you for this visit at the office, but we'll arrive early so we can do that in the car."

"Of course, I'm afraid I haven't prepared anything."

"That's natural, this is a very informal meet-and-greet with some residents. We will eventually ask you to introduce your continent and yourself on more formal occasions, but we can work up to those."

Gina also needed time to improve her Djanian language skills, thought Rngal. Gina had all of the day-to-day greetings at full proficiency and used them with excellent timing and accuracy. Greetings were a very important part of Djanian interactions. So, it was easy to overestimate Gina's ability, but when it came to times when she had to create new phrases and use a broader vocabulary, Gina still struggled. It didn't help that some sounds were impossible for her. Most of the paperwork yesterday had been translated by Brtann into Nülandish and, with the few documents that he hadn't gotten to, it had taken Gina much longer to go through them.

In her previous life, Rngal had been a translator and interpreter, she knew better than most how hard you had to work to get full proficiency in a languages as different as Nülandish and Djanian. She hoped that Gina would be up for the challenge. Rngal had not known many humans willing to make that investment.

"Today I will take you around the town centre, I will introduce you. You don't have to do much, but if you can say the normal greetings that should be fine. I'm afraid we will need to repeat that a lot today, so I hope you're ready to be patient."

"Absolutely, Denma was clear that this was part of the role. I have also mostly prepared the self-introduction presentation. I think I would just need help with explaining some of the final elements properly in Djanian."

"I can help with that. We can work on it at the office. I guess we'll also need to customise it to different audiences. After all, the presentation for the business owners will be different than the one for school children."

"Yes, I'd like your help with that too."

"We should also begin some introductory lessons to Nülandish as well."

"I'm not a language expert! But I can try."

"Luckily, I am a language expert." Rngal said with a wink, a human trait that she'd learned to mimic when working closely with humans in Prancinia.

"Really? Tell me more."

"In Prancinia, I worked as a translator for many years. I have a few degrees in linguistic studies, it's one of the reasons I was suitable for this role."

"I bet. It sounds like you might be more qualified than me for this job."

"But nowhere near as authentic." Rngal said with another wink and Gina chuckled.

On good terms, they got out of the vehicle and started the first visit. Rngal was right: it was a tedious day of greetings with people of varying importance.

Gina was exhausted by the end of the day, but they had managed to cover a third of the town in just the first day. Most had been open minded and Rngal had to admit that it was hard not to like Gina. Denma had made an excellent choice.

On the drive back to the town hall, Gina asked, "So what's the plan for tomorrow?"

"Same thing, I'm afraid, only this time with the schools. You'll get to meet the town's children."

"Sounds like I'll be a minor celebrity if today is anything to go by."

"I'm glad to hear that you don't mind it. This is the job for now. We may get into more depth in a few months' time, but, in the beginning, the goal is simply letting them get used to you and see you as an everyday part of the community."

23

Dead-end Forest, Hunter

The Guardian lunged forward again, but his punches had more power in them this time. As the battle continued, Hunter gave support to Rowan as he fought the Guardian at full strength. But Hunter hardly made any effort.

Hunter started to understand the difference in power, as he continued to support Rowan in the battle. He felt much stronger than the other two. The other two were absorbed in the battle and didn't notice Hunter's withdrawal.

Rowan landed a punch and half of the Guardian's body flew to bits. The Guardian jumped away from Hunter and Rowan. It needed a few seconds to heal its body, Rowan needed to catch his breath, after a moment he ran towards the Guardian again.

As the two were exchanging blows, Hunter watched from the side. It almost looked like Rowan could go neck and neck with the Guardian. But the Guardian had more experience, and this gave him the advantage in the fight with Rowan. Four arms also make a huge difference in close combat. Rowan fell to the ground, the Guardian who was standing looked down at him. Just as Rowan collapsed, Hunter ran forward to protect his new friend.

Hunter began with lightning-quick strikes of his sword, hacking away at the Guardian. The Guardian jumped back trying to escape, but Hunter was too quick. With deadly focus, Hunter continued his attack. He didn't notice, but at a certain moment, he lit up with blue flames, making his blade burn hotter than the sun.

Hunter charged at full speed to the Guardian, his sword sliced the Guardian to pieces, causing small explosions as the burning blade made contact with the Guardian.

In just minutes, all that was left of the Guardian was his head that shouted "Impossible! A Tyrant like me getting beaten by a couple of kids! This can't be!" The Guardian's head soon burned down to ashes.

Hunter worried for a second that the flames might burn down the entire forest, including Rowan, but then remembered his training. His grandpa had taught him, in theory, how to control a fire of his own making. He calmed his mind and willed the flames to die down. When he opened his eyes again, the fire was gone. Rowan, who was unconscious after the fight, woke up. Hunter was relaxing next to a charred stump of a tree nearby.

"Are you ok?" Hunter asked.

"I'll live. It'll take a hell of a lot more than that to keep the Frithe clan down for long. Did I mention? Our Talent is extreme durability. Mostly," Rowan looked around, "What the hell? Who burned the forest down? Where is the Guardian?" Rowan asked, sitting up.

"Where should I begin? You were unconscious for two hours and I killed the Guardian." Hunter answered.

"You were able to kill that thing?"

"Yes, I killed him. He was strong but it wasn't that hard." Hunter said. "Rowan, let me ask you something. What did the guardian mean when he said Superior and stuff like that?"

“Wait, don't tell me you don’t know about the Classes. Are you sure you’re from the Veronn clan?” Rowan said.

Hunter looked blank.

“Okay, let me explain, in Thaedim, Classes rank warriors, the lower the Class the stronger the person. There are six Classes. Soldier Class are people that are stronger than the average, so they can take on maybe four or five average guys. Constant Class are people that can cause a lot of damage. Superior Class can fight a large number of people. Tyrant Class are a threat to a city, so the police can't handle them. Destroyer Class can cause huge damage that can blow cities away. They pose a threat to a whole country. And lastly, we have the Dominion Class. It's the strongest out of all the classes, only six creatures have been able to get the title Dominion.”

A memory floated into Hunter’s mind. His grandpa was training him at home:

“Hunter, why won’t you listen to me? This is important.”

“It’s boring, I don’t care about how strong others are.” an eight-year-old Hunter complained.

“How will you ever be able to survive on Thaedim if you can’t even remember the Classes?”

“What's the big deal, Grandpa?”

Hunter’s grandpa sighed, “Listen, our clan is the strongest clan from the time of the Thaedim War.”

“The Thaedim War?”

“Give me strength!” His grandpa muttered. “The two-hundred-year war on Thaedim against the demons!” His grandpa huffed.

Back in the present, Hunter said, "Hmm, I might have heard about that somewhere. What rank are you?"

"I'm Superior but am planning on getting much stronger. What about you?"

"I don't know."

"I guess you can find out later. But I heard that after Superior it becomes hard to get a higher ranking. I've been here six months and I'm still trying to level up, before going to the Eternal Garden."

"Where do the Awakened fit in this ranking?" Hunter asked.

"Are you kidding?" Rowan stared hard at Hunter, whose face was genuinely curious. "It depends on the person, but the most powerful of the Awakened rank between Destroyer and Dominion."

"Which one was Dominion again?"

"I don't have the time for this. My head is killing me, I'm going to sleep." Rowan moved to his tent.

"Just wait till we get to the Eternal Garden, I'll get you some benthe root, best painkiller there is." Hunter grinned.

Rowan rolled his eyes and went to sleep, not long after Hunter also slept

24

Prancinia, Brtann

Five years ago, the year 6098

Brtann turned his attention from Rngal across the aisle and over the respective bins to Danica. In perfect Nülandish he said, "Good day, how is your search going?"

Rngal's shock was palpable, though Danica, as usual, noticed nothing.

After years of studying, Rngal had managed to master some of the human syllables that she heard him pronouncing perfectly. Danica hadn't noticed a thing and could not tell anything was amiss, the only idea that floated into her brain was, I should have hired him as my translator.

"Sadly, today is not a success. And on your end?"

Rngal listened, fascinated, her linguist's brain was absorbing the flow of conversation, the way Danica had skipped the greeting would be the height of rudeness. But Brtann did not seem disturbed.

"About the same." He inflected the words with a bit of humour, to open a door for a warmer interaction. He was curious about Danica. Humans were rare in this part of Prancinia. Taking a gamble, he asked, "What brings you here?"

"Work, and you?"

"The same, in fact. What do you do?"

"I'm in the incubator business, always looking for a new idea to support to market." Danica said, her eyes shifting to his gauntlets.

Brtann followed her obvious interest. "Ah, aren't we all," he said and casually picked up another gadget from the box and manipulated its features effortlessly. She seemed hypnotised.

Brtann had found his investor.

After that first encounter, Danica and Brtann got along quite well. Brtann was probably most taken with Danica's tenacious conviction that his wife's invention was a success and her desire to produce it on a mass scale. She saw Brtann and Lnore's vision.

Once Danica had found her product to invest in, Rngal was freed from many of her translator duties. At this point, she was the most knowledgeable Djanian about Sunnico's business, and she was a trusted long-time companion to Danica. Quickly, Rngal was brought in as Danica's second in command for the Sunnico tech hub. Rngal started getting more autonomy to work on behalf of Sunnico in Djania.

25

Ypare, Gina

Over the next month Gina came to terms with the reality of her dream job. She felt that she was somewhere between a prop and a language-learning app. Some days, she and Rngal would visit residents, where Gina's job was to be friendly, but not too friendly, so that they could get their first experience of meeting a human. This far into the countryside, it was rare for any of them to have seen humans anywhere but on trips to Prancinia, which was by far the largest concentration of humans in Breeland, but even there, they numbered among the thousands, surrounded by millions of breesians.

Gina did a good job with the greetings, which served her well. She'd almost memorised her self-introduction presentation, which Rngal had helped her optimise in Djanian. Together, they'd developed basic Nülandish classes for both adults and children.

Gina's Djanian was improving by the day, she had done well in progressing past the formal greetings within the first month. Now, she was making efforts to remember details of as many people as she could so that she could pick up the conversation the next time they met. It was one way to keep the repetitive nature of her job at least a little challenging and engaging.

Most of the staff at the town hall had warmed to her, and barely noticed her coming and going. She'd made a few acquaintances. But Nkano never changed his view of her.

Brtann and Rngal, both having known a fair number of humans in the past, were impressed by her dedication. They saw that the government programme might just be a success. Gina had also brought some liveliness and interest into what had become a tedious existence for both.

The more time Gina spent with Brtann the clearer it was that he had lived on Nüland, and for a very long time. He seemed more comfortable with her than with the other Djanians around him. He didn't seem to have many friends, though Rngal and he did seem quite close. Gina had wondered if it might be a romantic connection, but Brtann mentioned once that he was married. Gina had never met or even heard the name of Brtann's wife.

Rngal had a more traditionally Djanian way about her, but it was clear that she enjoyed spending time with Gina too.

Gina kept up with news from Nüland and messaged her family back home. She didn't have any news from Hunter but had managed to catch a news story on one of the only Nülandish channels that was broadcast this far into Djania. It mentioned the Raven District in Redall and the drug problem there, even some deaths from junkies trying to get their fix. She wondered whether Hunter was still there and though she hoped he wouldn't get caught up in that, but knowing him, he was probably right in the middle of it.

On one of her first weekends in Ypare, and without any other options for what to do in the countryside, Rngal had invited Gina to a monthly market in Ypare. Gina had loved it; it reminded her of the Djanian market back home, although this was smaller. There were some accessory stalls that she'd enjoyed visiting. It had been a good day with Rngal, and Gina marked her calendar so that she'd be sure to go again the following month.

26

Dead-end Forest, Hunter

It was morning, Hunter and Rowan continued walking through Dead-end Forest. It wasn't as threatening as they'd thought. After that first battle, it was pretty smooth for them: there were only a few creatures that attacked, but none as strong as the Guardian.

As they thought they were reaching the end of the forest, they encountered the ruins of a castle. The castle itself was almost completely destroyed, only a couple of towers were still standing. In the centre of the castle's courtyard, there was a statue of a knight. The statue was tall and held a sword over its shoulder. At the bottom of the statue there was an old carving of a few words. Hunter read the words out loud, "Krelin the Undefeated."

"Shit Hunter! You can read Thaedish!?"

Hunter shrugged. Then the ground started rumbling. Hunter and Rowan looked around.

"Hunter, what did you do?!" Rowan shouted.

"Nothing! I just read a few words on the statue."

A blast of energy came from the statue. They were thrown back. The statue was different than before. It was moving as if it were alive; in its right hand, the broad sword that had been resting on its shoulder was pointing towards them, ready to slice its enemies. Hunter took action and tried to slice the statue to pieces. The statue blocked his attack with immense speed. The two fought, Rowan, who couldn't do anything, watched the two fight each other. He could see that Hunter was much stronger than him.

As the fight continued, the blue flames started to glow around Hunter like before. Krelin was stronger than the Guardian. The sound of their swords clashing echoed through the trees as Hunter's blue-flamed strikes collided with the statue's unyielding defence. Krelin's eyes glowed with an ominous light, and its movements became more fluid, as if it was learning from Hunter's attacks. It countered his every move, forcing Hunter to go all out.

Hunter realised that Krelin's ability was learning and adapting. He couldn't let this fight go on for much longer; otherwise, the statue would learn all his moves and be able to counter them.

Hunter knew what he had to do to beat the statue, he shouted "Rowan take cover in the castle."

Rowan ran towards the castle. The statue noticed, and tried to stop Rowan but Hunter blocked it. Rowan found a place to take cover deep in the castle in the basement.

After Hunter was sure he gave Rowan enough time to take cover, he started a furious attack on the statue. He swung his blade, and it unleashed a huge explosion covering the whole area in flames, there was no trace of the statue.

"Well Krelin, I guess you aren't undefeated anymore." Hunter said and promptly passed out.

27

Redall, Brtann

Five years ago, the year 6098

When Brtann returned from Djania he was unusually enthusiastic.

He came into the workshop via the back door and placed his suitcases on the floor as Lnore set aside her tools.

She nuzzled him warmly. Her nose twitched; she could sense his agitation. She stepped back: “What is it?”

“I may have done it.”

“Done what?”

“Found a supplier that could manufacture your gauntlets in Djania.”

Lnore’s ears flattened. In her vision, her gauntlets would be made in Rominore. The investment of tech and jobs in a skilled sector would help bring her country out of poverty and reduce its dependence on Djania. She didn’t want her invention making Djanians richer.

Brtann was breathless, "They are all set up for it, the company is a human one, but has headquarters in both Prancinia and here in Redall. They're called

Sunnico and they've recently supplied the casinos around here with the latest in gambling games and slot machines. Okay that's not great. But Danica told me that they are looking to broaden the product range, get out of gambling and offer more mainstream products. Which is where your gauntlets come in. With the breesian market there and the diaspora here, they're convinced that this is a mainstream success that they can't miss out on. While I was in Djania, Danica brought me to the Sunnico tech hub. It's a huge campus with R&D side-by-side ultra-modern factories. So far, the focus was on gambling technology, but it seemed to me that they have the ability to shift over to the production of gauntlets because of some work they've done on gambling consoles with gauntlets for breesian audiences."

"Ah."

"They've already asked to see the specs and a blueprint, but I wanted to talk to you about it."

He could tell that she was deeply hesitant.

"I'm not sure how to say this, but I'd hoped that we could find a way to invest in Rominore and bring an opportunity to people that would thrive on this kind of investment. In Djania, this would be just another product. But in my country, it could bring communities out of poverty."

"Lnore, love, I want that too. But we're running out of cash. The store is barely covering our costs at this point, and we don't have the capacity. I've been trying to find investors, and this is the best deal we've gotten. Sunnico's determination to get out of gambling means that they're willing to let you keep the patent. You'll own the rights to the design, and, when we have the profits, we can move production to wherever we want."

"I don't like it."

"Look, how about this? We offer them a modified version of your gauntlets. We lose the weight carrying function. Make them comfortable, with the dexterity of human hands. No more, no less. That's already a huge improvement on what's currently available in the market. Danica is human and will likely not question something she understands. We can keep the full version for ourselves, for when we can expand out on our own."

"A modified version…" Lnore mused, "Going back to version 3.2... I think I have the specs around here." The current version was 5.8. She stayed quiet for a moment, then "Greg is a problem. He's seen it all."

Brtann could see the wheels turning in his wife's mind: it might just fly. "Greg's with us, we'll figure that out."

Her ears tentatively turned forward, "Okay, let's explore this." She moved into the workshop again and pulled out a case for gauntlets. She opened the case and presented her latest development: gauntlets with full human dexterity, enhanced grip, weight carrying feature and also razor-sharp claws. Every innovation into one pair. "While you were away, I got to thinking, you might need an upgrade," she said quietly.

Brtann was speechless, part of him was horrified that she was so worried about him that she felt this was the only way. Part of him was astounded at the gleaming gauntlets before him. Most of the time, gauntlets were bulky, cumbersome and the controls were finicky. But not these, they would bond seamlessly to his hands and work with ruthless efficiency. He itched to try them on.

Brtann slid his fingers into the gauntlet his wife had made. He didn't need words; he clenched his fists a few times and swiped viciously at the air in front of him. He raised himself to his full height. With these gauntlets he was a predator. He could face the threats the humans threw at him.

28

Ypare, Gina

Gina dug her toes into the thick rugs that covered the floor in her flat, she had become a full convert to the lush floor coverings and had embraced the Djanian rituals to care for their rugs.

She'd started her second month and was ready for a break, a visit to Prancinia. Though her airship had landed in Prancinia, she'd had only enough time to transfer onto the high speed rail network, and the rail terminal connected directly with the airship docking station. She'd been hinting to Brtann that she would make the arrangements for a trip to Denma Corp's Djanian headquarters. She wondered if she might see Montel again, even though he was clearly far too important to care about her. She'd begun thinking about what she could do after this 1-year contract ended. Might she relocate to Prancinia?

Her workdays had become monotonous. She had started to be seen as the 'local foreigner', a friendly oddity that did not require much comment on but needed to be shown around often enough so as not to be forgotten and lose the progress they had managed to make so far.

Although her Djanian grammar and vocabulary was improving, her pronunciation had stalled. She could not achieve certain low growls that were the commonest way to express assent. Each time she tried, the Djanians around her thumped their tails, in amusement.

Market day had come around again and this time Rngal was not able to join her, so Gina went alone to visit the market stalls.

She'd decided to wear casual clothes and not the dress code determined by Denma. It was early autumn and the cooler weather had yet to settle in, so she was wearing a short-sleeved summer dress as she browsed the aisles. Though some locals still stared at her, most let her get on with her browsing undisturbed. On the weekends, she tended to still wear her Rominore bracelet. She knotted it clumsily without the skill of a trained breesian.

She was engrossed at a stall that sold jewellery making supplies when she felt a cold metal gauntlet clamp painfully onto her wrist.

"Ow!" Gina yelped in sudden pain as the gauntlet tightened and twisted her wrist. She was yanked from the stall into the busy walking path. Gina remembered herself "This one asks why she is being treated like this!" She called out to her yet-unseen attacker.

The crowd parted, and she saw that it was Nkano and two other Djanians that she did not know. Maybe they were from another town, Gina thought randomly as Nkano's grip tightened, yanking her arm upward, seemingly he was interested in her arm.

"This one will examine your wrist, pet." He sneered at her.

"Someone was right," said Nkano's unknown companion, "That is a Rominore symbol."

"Yes, little pet," Nkano's expression changed, mocking Gina, "Why is someone wearing a Free Rominore banner in a Djanian market? Ypare does not accept such symbols in our midst."

"This one finds it beautiful. It was found in Nüland, this one does not know Rominore."

"This one thinks the pet has gone beyond her station and must be punished. It is clear that someone's handlers are not disciplining someone properly." Nkano's teeth flashed, and Gina was reminded of breesians' carnivorous heritage that had left them with wickedly sharp canines that could easily snap human bones. In a movement that she could hardly register, a claw came out from the gauntlet that gripped her wrist and slipped under her bracelet, ripping it in half. The bracelet slid to the ground, beads shattering as they hit the tile floor.

Then Nkano and his cronies were gone. The attack had taken seconds and was over in a flash. Gina looked at her wrist, it was red and swollen. She was sure it would be sprained, but it didn't seem broken. She started shaking. But she was alone, surrounded by Djanians that had either not seen or not cared enough to get involved.

Gina forced herself to stay calm and left the market, trying not to run. She managed to get back to her flat and lock the door. She leaned on the closed door and took a few deep breaths as tears came into her eyes.

She wrapped her wrist in gauze that she found in a first aid kit in her flat, hoping that if she immobilised it, it would stop some of the pain that suddenly hit her.

29

Dead-end Forest, Hunter

When Hunter woke up, Rowan was putting out the flames around him. Hunter closed his eyes and concentrated on putting out the flames. They disappeared in moments.

“What the hell Hunter, that was you?! Also, did you notice? You were glowing, it was like blue flames or something. Is that a Veronn clan thing?”

“Uh no, not normally. We can’t be burned though, that’s a Veronn thing.” Hunter rubbed his forehead where a massive headache had taken over. “This is gonna sound weird, but I think I might be Awakening…”

“No way! That’s great, that’s why you came to Thaedim, right? You can go home.” Rowan sounded cheerful.

“Not exactly, I need to get to the Eternal Garden, I could use some benthe tea right about now.”

“When you were fighting with the statue, I explored the castle basement a bit, there was a treasury down there, still filled with gold coins and jewels. Since we defeated the statue, and there doesn’t seem to be anyone else around, I’d say that the treasure’s ours. Want to go see it?”

“Maybe in a minute, I think I’ll rest a bit more first.”

They spent two more nights in the castle, until Hunter felt back to normal. It took another two nights in the forest and then finally made it through to the other side, with as much treasure as they could carry.

"I wonder if it's called Dead-end Forest because all the creatures there want to kill you and that it takes days to get through it," said Hunter.

"Hmm, who knows? But I bet for lots of clan members, it was a dead end to *their* trip to Thaedim," said Rowan.

30

Redall, Brtann

Five years ago, the year 6098

Lnore began to prepare for the deal with Sunnico. She'd found the plans for an earlier version of her gauntlets.

Version 3.2 had been a breakthrough for Lnore, when she had finally created a gauntlet that could mimic human dexterity and strength of grip. It had been the gateway to her innovations with the weight bearing functions and more.

She returned to the product specs and altered them a little, reducing the possibility for innovation by dismantling the receptors that had eventually allowed her to innovate further. The blueprints for a version suitable for Sunnico took a few weeks to develop. After that, she needed to create a corresponding pair of prototype gauntlets. This added another few months to the timeline.

Brtann knew that Danica was getting restless, but he kept her at bay with a number of excuses.

Until the day Danica arrived at their shop. Their time had run out.

Greg, who had been a fan of Danica and idolised her career path, met her at the door, a little starstruck as she walked in. There had been whispers as she'd alighted from her vehicle to walk into the store.

Danica was a minor celebrity in Redall, having grown up in obscurity to achieve the highest levels of education and had climbed the ranks of Sunnico, expanding the tech arm of the business.

When she'd first been hired, 20 years ago, Sunnico had been a small pharma company with its major investment in one or two pharmaceutical products. Her role had been to optimise the processes in the drug development process.

But they hadn't counted on Danica's knack for business development. Almost single-handedly, with the approval of a far-sighted manager, she'd grown the tech side of the business. Like Greg, she'd also been fascinated with Djania when she was young, she'd been determined to find a way to link Djanian tech to Sunnico's products. She didn't bother to learn enough about the breesian continent to realise there were other countries than Djania. Like many on the human continent, she thought all breesians were Djanian.

Danica was a scrappy businesswoman, who didn't turn her nose up at anything without giving it a chance first. This was how gambling machines became the first products that Sunnico manufactured in Djania. Objectively, Danica was fascinated by the psychology behind the "game" as she saw it. She rarely bothered to concern herself with the consequences of what being addicted to her products meant for people in the Raven District.

She was for Sunnico to expand away from gambling tech into more palatable businesses and made sure that the Sunnico name stayed off the gambling machines and games.

"H-hello" Greg stammered as he tripped over his feet to welcome her. His arm swung widely, almost hitting a few products, "To what do we owe this honour?"

Danica looked at Greg, he was a skinny kid, just out of school, scruffy around the edges, but clearly keen to do a good job and aware of who she was. She decided to play nice.

“Hello, Greg -is it?- I think Brtann mentioned you.” Greg flushed with happiness that he may have somehow been brought to Danica’s attention. “Might you know where I can find Brtann?” Danica asked, her eyes scanning the shop and noting the eclectic and ingenious product selection.

“Y-yes, let me find him for you, please wait here.”

Greg rushed to the back, through the short hallway between the workshop and the store. In the workshop, Brtann and Lnore were speaking softly in Djanian.

He burst into the room and blurted, “It's Danica! She's here, and she's asking for you.”

Brtann and Lnore's eyes met, and with a slight twitch of the ears, they agreed that it was time. Time to show the blueprints, time to sign the deal.

Together they went back into the shop.

31

Mendani, Hunter

After leaving the forest Hunder and Rowan came to a lake. The water looked clean, so they stopped for a break. The next city, Mendani, wasn't far away. They arrived still in the afternoon, the city was filled with all different species, including humans and breesians.

They were surprised to see a city on Thaedim where this was possible.

“I guess some warriors decide to stay here instead of returning to Nüland after their training. Maybe the demons aren’t all bad?” Rowan said to Hunter as they walked through the streets.

They tried to go shopping, since they needed to stock up on food, but when they tried to pay with the coins from the castle ruins, it seemed that they might be cheated by not having the local currency. Rowan suggested that they look for a place where they could trade some of the gold for money. They soon found a stall where they were able to exchange gold for cash.

“I wonder how much we’ll need to get. We don’t want to spend all of our money here,” said Rowan

“We did get a lot of treasure from Dead-end Forest, so we should be ok for the rest of the journey.” Hunter said.

A troll appeared behind the counter, “How can I help you?” He seemed much more articulate than either Hunter or Rowan had been led to expect from Thaedim’s demons.

“Were looking to trade some gold for money,” said Hunter

“That’s what we do. But before you guys can do that, could you first fill in this document?”

Hunter and Rowan, taken aback by the civilised nature of this Thaedian, filled in the document and handed it back to him. The troll looked through the document.

“A Superior and an Awakened!” said the troll.

Rowan looked at Hunter with surprise. Hunter shrugged, he hadn’t known how to fill in the form, even though he wasn’t sure he qualified as Awakened.

“Is there a problem?” Hunter asked.

“N-no problem, but it's just we haven't had an Awakened in a while. Most of the people these days who come to this city are either Soldiers or Constants.”

“Really? But this is Thaedim,” Hunter said.

“Yes, but this part of Thaedim isn’t so dangerous.” The troll paused breifly, “oh, there *is* someone who ranks Tyrant in Mendani. But I doubt you’ll encounter her.”

“Her?”

“Her name is Vraya. She was the strongest in this city before you guys arrived.”

After that, the troll produced two large pouches of money. They left the stall and headed out to the city.

Since they didn’t have any business in Mendani, they wanted to leave as soon as possible and continue on to the Eternal Garden. They went through an alley.

"You keep mentioning benthe root or benthe tea, what is that anyway?"

For once, Hunter had more knowledge about Thaedim than Rowan. "It is a strong painkiller, and it helps wounds heal faster too. My clan always harvests some benthe to bring back. My mom even cultivated a benthe garden once, but she burned it down without telling me why."

"I'm not sure what plant I'll get to prove I went to the Eternal Garden, but benthe sounds good to me." Rowan replied. It seemed that if it wasn't about fighting, or Frithe clan honour, he didn't pay much attention.

They started talking about the legends of the Eternal Garden. As they reached the end of the alley something flew by, right next to them at full speed.

"What the… is that a drone?!"

32

Redall, Brtann

Five years ago, the year 6098

“Danica,” Brtann called, “It’s wonderful to see you.”

“Brtann, yes, it's been too long. I'm so pleased to see you in the Raven District at your very own store. Allow me to compliment you, this is really an impressive assortment.” Without looking, Brtann could feel Lnore gloat a little, always pleased to be proven correct.

Not wanting to show her into the workshop, where evidence of the various iterations of the gauntlets lay scattered about, they invited her to their flat to speak privately. When they were all seated comfortably Danica continued.

“I know it’s a little unorthodox, but I thought I’d check up on you, it’s been a few months now since we spoke in Prancinia, and I wondered if our deal was still on the table.”

“Of course, as I told you the gauntlets are not mine to sell, of course, so allow me to introduce you to my wife Lnore. She is the brains behind the gauntlets.”

Lnore, always more cautious than Brtann, made a minor gesture with her ears to acknowledge that she was the inventor. Danica missed the gesture entirely and stared blankly at Lnore, who, unlike Brtann and his eye-catching grey fur, looked more like other breesians. His exceptional colouring had meant that Brtann stood out in Danica's mind as exceptional among the Djanians. His wife, however, did not live up to Danica's skewed expectations.

To be polite, she nodded at Lnore, but then continued, speaking to Brtann. She assumed that the Djanians did not -as a whole- speak Nülandish whether they lived in Djania or Liunia. "I wanted to arrange a visit to Sunnico HQ, we have all the paperwork ready, and our team is itching to get a look at the blueprints and prototype. I don't suppose you'd have something to show me today that I could take back to them. You know, in good faith."

Lnore's tail twitched with annoyance, Brtann caught the gesture and attempted damage control.

"Ah -good faith- you say, indeed we've kept you waiting, but we wanted to be certain that the product spec and prototype would be in a format that is most suited for your development team. You see Lnore has been working on her own for the most part and hasn't had to consider other developers yet. It took a little time to -ah- make the instructions -ah- readable outside our lab. I thought there was agreement on this point..."

"I understand that," Danica quickly added, "but my management has started to question this venture, and if we don't move fast, we may lose their good will."

"Good will?" Lnore interrupted. "I'm afraid I don't understand. Without my gauntlets you don't have another viable product option on the table for shifting Sunnico production into the mainstream. I believe goodwill must go both ways. As the developer, I need my time to prepare accordingly."

Danica's attention swivelled from Brtann to Lnore; perhaps she'd underestimated this pair. She tried for damage control, "You're right. We need you." She took a breath, "but you need us too. We can make these gauntlets a household name, desired by every Djanian-"

“I think you mean breesian.” Lnore inserted.

Danica waved the distinction away, “Yes, exactly. So, we need your input and ideally your signatures on the contract as soon as possible.”

Brtann, with the skill and charm of a salesman saw his opening, “And you will indeed have it. Top of our agenda. Let’s meet next week at Sunnico HQ with our blueprints. And of course, our best gauntlets to sign those contracts.”

Danica wearily brought her attention back to Brtann, “Sounds good. In one week, are we agreed?”

“That’s perfect,” Brtann said smoothly. And escorted her out.

33

Ypare, Gina

The next day at work, Brtann noticed Gina's wrist and insisted she go to the hospital. As he drove her there, he managed to get the story out of her. He stayed with her, knowing that Ypare's medical infrastructure was not designed for humans. He knewn well enough of what she might encounter from his time on Nüland and visiting hospitals that weren't designed for breesians. When the doctor announced that her wrist was sprained, Brtann's ears twitched backward angrily; his gauntlets clenched into fists.

When they returned to the office, a splint wrapped around Gina's wrist, Rngal was waiting. She looked up quizzically when they came in.

"Brtann, Gina, where have you been? We were due at the school two hours ago!"

"You need to hear this, Rngal." Brtann said and gently guided Gina to a chair. Gina, miserably, repeated the story. But as she finished talking, rather than sending her away, Brtann and Rngal included her in the discussions of what should happen next.

"Nkano must be punished. He's never liked humans and was just waiting for a chance to catch her alone. We need to make an example out of this." Brtann was seething.

"Brtann, no I-I don't want to make things worse. What if I bump into him again? Are you and Rngal supposed to be my full-time minders? No thank you." Gina said.

"Gina's right, Brtann, there's nothing we can do about cretins like Nkano, he's not going to change and punishing him will only increase his hatred. It was during a weekend, and he could claim that the bracelet was a provocation. He is probably just as violent and territorial when it comes to people from Rominore." Rngal turned to Gina, "In no way does this change that what he did was awful and should not have happened, but that bracelet gives him plausible cause in the eyes of some of the people around here."

Brtann's gauntlets remained clenched as Rngal and Gina went out for the next appointment of the day.

Brtann walked with them past the entryway and co-working space. He saw Nkano smirk as Gina walked by. He did not react. Yet.

A week later, Gina was leaving work as she passed by Brtann's office, she called out, "This one leaves now," the traditional greeting at the end of the day.

"This one calls you in."

Gina was already on her way to the door when the unexpected response came. With an internal groan she moved towards the door and slid it open. Brtann crouched at his low desk, a tablet in front of him.

"Yes, Brtann?" She returned to Nülandish.

"I've had a message from Denma Corp. Montel will be in Prancinia in two weeks. He's asked that you come to see him while he's there."

Gina kept the frown from her face, she wondered how much the incident with Nkano had inspired this sudden summoning to Prancinia, while she'd been trying to arrange a visit for weeks now, had Brtann pulled some strings? Brtann and the Djanian government were clients. They should not get information about her or make such descisions for her.

“We’ll go together. It’s been too long since I’ve been to the city.” Brtann said

She blinked her acceptance of this suggestion, as Djanians would, rather than nodding her head. She accepted that exactly what she had wanted had finally happened, if not exactly *how* she'd wanted it to happen. Her wrist was healing well and would be fine in a few weeks. She did not want constant supervision from Brtann and Rngal, but she'd noticed that over the past week, they had been hovering around her. They had only left her alone once she was back at her flat.

The night before their trip, Nkano had both his wrists broken. This was a horrific injury for breesians: it stopped them from being able to wear gauntlets and left them almost entirely without the use of their hands for weeks, if not months. Nkano refused to say how the injury happened.

PART 4 - DEFEAT

Interlude 3

"It took me years to assemble this evidence, and now no one will look at it. I've tried with the authorities here in Grantan, and also over the border in Liunia, but no one seems to care. Was it all for nothing?" Hunter's mom was saying to his dad. Hunter, now thirteen, had recently started his lessons on stealth. He was all too eager to lurk around corners and eavesdrop on conversations. It was a new interest that frequently drove Gina crazy.

"It might be a sign that this isn't the right time." Talik replied.

"But that means it will keep happening, it's already been more than 14 years since I left, how much worse could it be now? I can't pretend I didn't see what I saw or forget how I contributed in the worst way."

"It's okay. You didn't know. I promise there will come a time when Sunnico will pay."

Hunter hovered outside the room for a moment, not sure what he was listening to. Rather than his usual tendency to jump in the room and reveal his stealthy approach, something told him his parents wouldn't be happy that he had listened in on this conversation. He moved silently away, leaving his parents to continue their conversation.

Hunter's fighting abilities were coming along well, he had recently started training with a short metal Veronn blade. He was quickly getting used to the heft of it, and the newly deadly nature of his sparring bouts. His book learning remained an uphill struggle. He seemed to forget most lessons as soon as they were over.

Neil had started looking forward to Gina's visits, because it seemed that she was the only one who could manage to get any knowledge into Hunter's hard head.

34

Mendani, Hunter

"Rowan! Check your bags!"

Rowan checked "Where's our money...? The drone!"

The drone was nearly out of sight, but Rowan picked up a rock and threw it at the drone with full force. He just barely missed. The drone flew away, Hunter and Rowan knew they had to get the money back. They asked a passer-by if they knew anything about drones.

"A drone? It must be Vraya's."

"Vraya. Can you tell me how to get to her?"

"Yes, but I recommend you stay away from her. I heard that she's very strong and once took down a hundred men. But if you guys are looking for her, she mostly hangs out near the breesian area."

Hunter and Rowan found a place to sit down and think their plan through.

"A drone," Rowan said shaking his head, "I learned that the last drones were put out of use when the Thaedim War ended. I never thought I would encounter a real one. I guess this means that we will have to fight to get our money back."

"Yeah,"

"Hunter, when we run into Vraya. Let me handle it. I want to get stronger, and I can't get stronger unless I beat someone stronger than me."

Hunter nodded.

They headed for the breesian area. The breesians looked at Rowan and Hunter with unwelcoming faces. A group of breesians came up to them.

"Well, well well, would you look at this? A couple of lost humans in our territory," said one of the breesians in Nülandish.

"We don't want any trouble. We're just looking for someone."

"Huh, looking for someone? Don't you know the situation you're in you stupid human?" said the breesian flexing his claw-tipped battle gauntlets.

"If you guys would drop all your stuff and money here, we might let you g…"

Rowan punched the breesian before he could finish his sentence. The breesian flew back crashing into a building. The other breesians looked shocked.

"What were you gonna do? Try and rob us? We happen to be a little upset since we were already robbed today. I'll ask you guys just once: do you guys know a woman called Vraya?" said Hunter

"Don't get ahead of yourself, you humans. We've got Soldiers and Constants on our side. So, you guys better get on your knees and…"

Rowan and Hunter both easily knocked out several of the breesians. The rest backed off.

"That was good warm up before we're gonna fight Vraya." said Rowan

"Yeah, you said you'd handle her, right? Don't let your guard down, she's a Tyrant. That's a rank higher than you."

"I know"

Out of the blue, a rocket launched towards them. Hunter and Rowan dodged but almost got blown away.

"I heard a couple of humans were looking for me," said a voice from beyond the explosion.

35

Redall, Brtann

Five years ago, the year 6098

Despite Brtann's enthusiasm for the deal with Sunnico and his hopes for its potential to change their lives, Brtann hesitated in the final moments. After what both he and Lnore could only feel was a visit meant to intimidate, he decided to take another look into Sunnico's portfolio. In Djania, Sunnico had a great tech hub that was primed to develop their gauntlets. But he couldn't ignore that the current purpose of those labs and factories was the production of gambling machines and software. He'd said to Lnore that this wasn't a reason to refuse the deal, but now he questioned that idea

As he continued investigating in the outskirts of Redall, where land was cheaper, he found Sunnico's pharmaceutical labs. It was a massive campus, the size of half a city, with high security; no one was getting in or out easily. Some of their big-name drugs were hugely impactful in pain relief, especially at the end of life. They'd also found ways to slow the flow of blood through the body, to reduce blood loss to major wounds. Both drugs were sold under their own brands. When he dug deeper, he found some evidence that the drug trials had been carried out under questionable circumstances, but much of that information was buried. Sunnico targeted most of their pharma products at humans, claiming that breesians' larger size and varied metabolism meant that the drugs were unstable. They didn't seem interested in offering medical benefits to his people.

In the Raven District, Brtann started to notice the number of casinos and gambling halls. In his research of Sunnico, he'd noticed that they distributed their gambling tech under several sub-brands. As he walked around the Raven District, he noticed that although each business seemed to have its own identity, they were all part of the Sunnico brand portfolio, from the high-end casinos to the dive bars with slot machines.

Sunnico seemed to own most of the Raven District.

Brtann began to wonder if the development of the Raven District had been for the greater integration and future vision of Redall, or if it had just been offered by the city government as a testing ground for Sunnico's latest products.

He began visiting the casinos, to see what their other product range offered. As a precaution, he began to wear the latest pair of gauntlets that Lnore had prepared for him on his investigations. He closed his gauntlets into fists when walking to make the claws less obvious.

On the surface, the casinos were clean and the gamblers more or less what you would expect from such a place. There was a mix of Raven District people, with both breesians and humans sitting at tables and slot machines.

On his first visit, nothing out of the ordinary happened, but his sensitive nose had picked up an odour that he didn't recognize, something earthy and oddly alluring.

In the week they still had before signing the contract, he kept visiting different Sunnico establishments, each of which had the bizarre smell, until finally, he arrived at a casino where the chemicals were flooding through the vents. The humans didn't seem to notice, but he saw the breesian gamblers leaning back and inhaling deeply. They were getting high. Brtann wasn't sure what to do, should he stay and investigate? Or get the hell out of there? He chose the latter.

Even after just a few short breaths, he was already feeling hazy. He tried shaking his head a few times but noticed his vision blurring, with odd shapes seeming to come out of nowhere. He stumbled back out onto the street, but the shapes kept chasing him. He swung his arms out to ward off the oncoming figures. The first two times the figures proved to be only in his imagination. The third time, he connected. He saw a human figure go flying.

That snapped him out of his haze.

36

Prancinia, Gina

Gina met Brtann and Rngal early the next morning at Ypare's only train station. At first, she didn't recognise them. In the place of the conservatively dressed town hall employees, now stood two fully urban Djanians. Both had shed their small-town identities.

Gina felt like she might be seeing them both as they truly were for the first time. Brtann wore a monochrome palette, showing off his grey fur in a sleek and calculated way. Rngal wore a complicated dress with intricate pleats and folds, she was a vibrant, colourful contrast to Brtann. Gina felt foolish for wearing her usual work uniform, in fact outfits like this were all she had packed for the trip to Prancinia. She cringed to herself, she wanted to match these stylish Djanians as they made their way to the capital.

The trio stood together on the platform of the tiny station, until a one-car train appeared. In the next junction, they exchanged their one-car train for a normal-sized train.

At the next, even bigger city, they transferred onto the high-speed light rail network that connected all the major Djanian cities. For the first time since arriving, Gina saw a handful of humans. She tried to make eye contact, but they did not seem to notice her. On the light rail, Gina again experienced the nausea that was typical of this kind of high-speed transport.

And then they arrived in Prancinia.

The Djanians never did anything by halves. Their capital was a super-modern hub with gleaming surfaces everywhere. The intent was to impress and intimidate. And it succeeded. Gina was too busy looking at all the sights to notice Brtann and Rngal's heightened scanning of the city around them.

"Brtann, this is amazing!" Gina said, while still taking everything in. The sights, sounds, and smells were tailored to Djanian's senses, and she was only getting half the experience that Brtann and Rngal had. Their ears thrummed with soft messages inviting them into shops. Their sensitive noses were tempted by the lingering smells from delicious street food vendors and restaurants. The bright lights and primary colours were adapted to the more limited range of colours that breesian eyes could decipher.

It was already evening so they decided to get a meal and head to their hotel for the evening. Rngal seemed to know the city best and directed them to an out-of-the-way restaurant which served both human and Djanian food. Gina savoured her meal.

They strolled through the busy streets to their hotel, Gina trailing behind Brtann and Rngal, eagerly drinking up the atmosphere.

She protested when they reached the hotel so soon. "But it's still early, everything is still open. I'd just like to window shop."

Rngal and Brtann held a wordless exchange. Gina had no reason to be cautious, she had no history here. Rngal indicated Gina could go with her tail.

Brtann and Rngal entered the hotel as Gina headed off into the night.

37

Redall, Brtann

Five years ago, the year 6098

Brtann could not tell if anyone had seen him. He wanted to see if the person was alright, but his mind would not think clearly. Without another thought, he ran. He arrived at the back door of his home. Sliding the door open, he collapsed on the floor. Lnore was in the workshop as usual, Greg was in the shop.

Lnore carried Brtann to their flat before anyone could notice the commotion. It was nearing dusk, but the shop was still busy with customers.

Brtann slept off the worst of the drug's effects and woke in the early evening.

Lnore's worried face was the first thing he saw.

"What happened?"

His mind wasn't clear, he remembered the casino, the chemicals, and then sending a human flying.

"It's Sunnico, they're drugging people in their casinos. That smell, that smell…" he stuttered, "And I … I didn't mean to hurt him."

"Hurt who?"

“I don’t know.”

“I can smell the chemicals on you, any breesian would be able to. You need to stay here. I'll go to investigate.”

“No!” Brtann tried to sit up. “We need to cut ties with Sunnico, there is something rotten there. I don't think they are planning to get out of the casino business, they want to use your gauntlets as a cover story, to hide what's going on. You know what I found out? There is a pharmaceutical hub that is at least as big as their tech hub in Djania, just outside of Redall. It seems that, along with the legal drugs, they are also developing illegal varieties too.” He knew he was babbling and that this didn't make sense, but he needed to say it out loud to get it out of his head. “But why in the casinos? Do they want to addict the gamblers to stay longer? Do they just give a taste so that they'll create a new market for their drugs?” He'd hit a wall in his feverish logic, and his brain was going fuzzy again.

A few hours later Brtann woke again. This time it was Greg that was with him. The store had long since closed. Brtann’s ears and nose did an investigation of the room. Lnore was not there.

He tried to sit up again.

“Whoa Brtann. You need more rest before you move again.” Greg gently pushed him back onto the couch. Brtann brought his hands up to ward off the touch, but Lnore had removed the gauntlets in his sleep, with only his own strength and feeble hands he could do little more than swat at Greg ineffectually.

“Where is Lnore?”

“She went out for supplies about an hour ago. She said she’d be back soon.”

“No. I need to get to her.” Brtann’s mind was confused, but he managed not to reveal what he’d learned about Sunnico.

Just then, Lnore came back. "Thanks Greg, it's ok, I've got him now. See you tomorrow." She sounded so calm, confusing Brtann.

Greg gave the pair a sunny smile. "I hope you feel better tomorrow, see you later."

Brtann sat up, the drug had left his system, with just a throbbing headache in its wake. Lnore made tea with added painkillers. She handed it to Brtann and watched him drink half before talking.

"I-I found out what happened. The authorities were all over it. It was a full crime scene. I tried to listen in. Luckily, I don't stand out in a crowd."

Brtann let that pass, knowing what she meant.

"It was not pretty, there was blood everywhere. Brtann he's dead, I'm sorry I know you didn't mean it."

Brtann ears flattened, and his eyes spun wildly. "What…?"

"I know" she reached for him, but her gauntlets flashed in the dim light. She pulled back, flicked the release switch.

She didn't watch as her life's work thudded to the floor.

38

Mendani, Hunter

"You're the guys that so carelessly left your money where my drone could find it. This shouldn't take long." Vraya appeared out of the smoke from the explosion.

Rowan could feel that she was strong, stronger than him. Vraya was breesian with two enormous gauntlets. Hunter looked at the gauntlets and knew that a normal person would be sent flying with one punch. But as trained fighters, he and Rowan were anything but normal. And Rowan wouldn't easily get blown away. Hunter thought Rowan had a chance of winning and stepped back from the fight.

Rowan jumped, closing the distance to Vraya, but she didn't seem shaken at all, so she didn't just depend on her machines. She seemed very comfortable with both close- and long-range combat. She tried to hit Rowan with a powerful punch. Rowan dodged out of the way. Rowan thought to himself that the gauntlets were a problem. They had a huge range, making it harder for him to dodge. He needed to destroy the gauntlets to win against her. Rowan launched himself forward again, going for a hard punch. Suddenly, Vraya's gauntlets hit him hard. Rowan flew back.

"What was that? The gauntlet moved like a rocket." Rowan exclaimed.

He saw an engine at the elbow of Vraya's gauntlet making her punches harder and faster. Rowan needed a second to recover.

“What, done already? I wouldn’t even call that a warm up,” Vraya flashed her teeth, amused.

Rowan caught his breath and was ready to fight again. Just as he got up, Vraya appeared and went for another punch. Rowan managed to dodge it. He aimed his next punch on the gauntlets, landing a solid hit.

“You bastard! you dented my gauntlets.” Vraya growled and hit him again.

Rowan got up. Even with his hardest punch all it left was a dent. He needed another method. He leapt over to where he had left his backpack, near Hunter. He reached in and pulled out a baton the length of his arm. He pressed a button and it extended into a spear taller than he was. This drew Hunter’s attention, he looked closely at the weapon and identified it as the Frithe clan’s signature weapon, the Skorpian spear.

Rowan ran in full speed towards Vraya and hit her with his spear. She blocked it and hit back. Rowan managed to scratch her shoulder with the spear. Vraya kept out of the way.

“You’re not bad of a fighter, guess I’ll need to get serious”.

Rowan's eyes widened; he'd been fighting full out, and she was just now going to get serious? Two drones appeared behind her. They were different from the one that stole the money. These drones were bigger, with guns and explosives. The drones aimed for Rowan. He took cover behind a thick stone wall. The drones started firing.

As the drones attacked, Vraya had a moment to wonder why Hunter wasn’t fighting. But she couldn’t focus on it for long, she turned her attention back to the battle she was already in.

The drones had shot so many bullets that the wall nearly fell over on Rowan.

When the drones stopped firing, he threw his spear. It flew at full speed towards Vraya. She was caught off guard. The spear was about to hit Vraya when one of her drones flew in front of her and took the hit, exploding into pieces in front of her. Rowan thought he might have had a chance to beat her, but the drones took the fight to the next level. Not only can they shoot at a target until death is confirmed, but also can be used as a shield.

This was the level of difficulty he expected from a Tyrant. If he were to beat Vraya, he needed to have a plan.

Meanwhile, Hunter stood back from the fight, his mind elsewhere. It had been months since he left his hometown. And, if he was right, he was in the process of being Awakened. The Veronn clan's Awakened had levelled several Thaedian cities in a week-long offensive that had been the key to victory in the war.

Rowan came up with a plan, but he needed to get his spear back in order to win this fight. Vraya grew bored of having her drones do all the work. She lunged forward and destroyed the wall Rowan was behind. Rowan had to rely on his martial arts training. Between Rowan and Vraya there was no way that Rowan could win, he was a rank lower and lacked the experience that she had.

She punched Rowan, and he flew into a house. She shot another rocket into the house where Rowan crashed. Vraya thought Rowan was dead, but the Frithe clan were nearly indestructible. Once the smoke cleared, he was gone. Vraya had lost sight of him. She turned around; he was running to get his spear. The last drone started shooting its remaining bullets in Rowan's direction. He managed to dodge the bullets and picked up his spear and stabbed it through the drone. Vraya didn't see that coming, she thought he was just another Superior but that wasn't the case. She realised he was strong, and if she wasn't careful, she might actually lose this fight.

"Let's see what else you've got," said Vraya.

After the two drones that Rowan had downed, four more of Vraya's drones came and surrounded the area. Vraya's gauntlet flashed red for a second and huge claws flexed from the fingertips.

“Guess I'm still no match for a Tyrant. Hunter! You can take care of it from here. This is it for me,” called out Rowan.

“No, I think you can still go a little more before you hit your limits,” Hunter said, still lost in thought.

Rowan didn't expect Hunter to turn him down. Vraya, aimed her huge gauntlet claws at Rowan.

Rowan tightened his grip on his spear. Vraya's drones aimed at Rowan. Hunter began watching the fight. Vraya gestured towards Rowan, and the drones started firing. Rowan started swinging his spear in a circular motion, so fast that it created a shield. Bullets hit the spinning spear like hitting a wall. But he couldn't keep it up for long, Rowan was losing speed, the technique needed a lot of stamina. Some bullets were starting to get through, one hit Rowan on the shoulder.

Rowan was on his last leg. He stopped swinging his spear and started running at the drones, destroying them one by one. He didn't notice that he'd been hit several times, it was like he couldn't feel the pain. As he destroyed the drones, they stopped shooting.

Rowan was wondering why the drones stopped attacking. A realisation came to him. He looked at the spot where he last saw Vraya. But she wasn't there. Suddenly he felt a huge change in atmosphere. He looked over his shoulder and saw Vraya not even a second away from him, she was ready to stab those claws right through him. Rowan didn't have the time to dodge, it was too late.

Faster than either Vraya or Rowan could grasp, Hunter had moved between them, his sword facing Vraya.

39

Prancinia, Gina

Gina knew she had to be on form for tomorrow's meeting at Denma, so she didn't want to go overboard but she couldn't help ducking in a few shops and gazing at the sparkling selection in front of her. Her attention was pulled towards an accessory shop that seemed to specialise in the woven, Rominore jewellery.

"Welcome" boomed the shopkeeper in Nülandish.

"This one is pleased to enter", Gina replied in Djanian.

The shopkeeper seemed amused, but replied in a Djanian accent that Gina did not recognize. "Someone is welcome."

"This one finds the necklace beautiful. Might I see this?" Gina asked, knowing it was rude to point, but also that her flat face made gesturing with her nose impossible, she tried to point with her chin to the necklace she had in mind.

"Ah, someone has exquisite taste! Does someone know about the necklaces?"

Gina's face remained neutral, "This one has had some encounters, they are from Rominore."

"Someone has good knowledge!" The shopkeeper seemed pleased, "And so someone must know of Rominore craftsmanship, since that is the origin of these necklaces."

"No, I -uh- this one doesn't know much more than that."

"Rominore is the nation to the west of Djania and it is this one's homeland. It creates the textiles, tapestries and rugs that make Djania so colourful. If it was not for Rominore, Djania would be a sterile, ugly place!"

Gina could see his pride in his country. Their rugs were famous, but in Nüland, the rugs and tapestries were all considered Djanian, and humans marvelled at the nation that could merge incredible technological achievements with astounding woven arts. She thought about her own thesis from just a year ago and how incorrect it had been, and how much she had learned since then.

"This one wants to know more about your land, but for now would like to please purchase this necklace."

The shopkeeper's tail thumped a few times on the floor in appreciation of her answer. She'd chosen an intricate weave of blues and purples with a flicker of gold thread running through it. The necklace was wider than her old one. The shopkeeper handed it carefully to her, and she looked at the price tag and gulped. But she'd been collecting a salary for a few months, with very little to spend it on. She handed the money over.

She wrapped it around her wrist twice, making it closer in size to a cuff. The shopkeeper expressed the same curiosity that the stall owner did back Grantan where she had gotten her first bracelet. He soon understood how she planned to wear it.

The shopkeeper gestured for her to hold out her wrist. She hesitated, looking at the ties of the bracelet, it looked too complex for even gauntleted Djanian -no- Rominore hands to manage. Not to be rude, she placed her uninjured arm forward.

With surprising dexterity, the shopkeeper managed the knot. There was an art to this too. She could not have done it herself but was eager to learn how, if there was ever an opportunity.

The shopkeeper stood back, admiring his handiwork. "Someone shines with this new accessory."

Gina realised he was genuinely touched that a human had appreciated his country's jewellery. She was very pleased that she'd insisted on exploring the city.

The next morning, Gina met Brtann and Rngal in the hotel's breakfast room. Brtann had been sure to find a hotel that would offer both human and Djanian food. Gina ate gratefully, after months of the small selection of edible foods for her in Ypare, this buffet was incredible.

They left the hotel just after daybreak, as Prancinia was waking up.

When they reached Denma Corp, Gina was surprised to see a building in such an aggressively human style. It was a vertical cement and metal brick in a city of organic buildings, mostly made of wood and glass. It seemed designed to make a very human point: that Denma were a force to be reckoned with.

She went inside. Brtann and Rngal had again been on high alert on the trip to Denma Corp, they had also noticed Gina's new bracelet and were monitoring her. Gina was beginning to understand the statement she was making by wearing it.

They sailed through security and whisked up to the 17th floor.

They entered into a waiting room. The furniture was set up for both breesians and humans. Gina took a seat, she saw Brtann and Rngal do the same.

Then, they were called in.

40

Redall, Brtann

Five years ago, the year 6098

When the last of the drug's effects wore off, Lnore started telling Brtann more about how the authorities had said that the victim seemed to be drugged before the incident that claimed his life. And how Brtann's distinctive colouring had been spotted as he stumbled home.

Brtann was a known member of the community with his role in their store.

"You're not safe here," was Lnore's quiet but definitive conclusion. She continued, "I think you're right. As insane as it sounds, it looks like Sunnico is trying to take over the Raven District and is combining their gambling machines and drugs to do so."

She continued: "Even if you weren't in control of yourself, you know how the authorities treat breesians if they've hurt a human. You'll be locked away. Unless…"

"Unless…?" Brtann echoed hopelessly.

"Unless we get you out of here. To Djania. You have contacts there, you can disappear."

“Wait -I- can disappear? What about you? Everyone knows we’re together. You aren’t safe here either.”

“I think I might be okay. Sunnico still wants my gauntlets. I will follow through on the deal. They need me to make their business look more legitimate, as a cover for what they are doing here. They can’t afford to let the authorities take me out of the equation.”

“No.”

“What choice do we have? We are up against a massive company or the authorities that are known to terrorise breesians that step out of line, even sometimes those that don’t.”

Brtann, defeated, prepared for a one-way trip to Djania.

PART 5 - INTERRUPTED

Interlude 4

Gina and her dad still visited the forges on a weekly basis. At fifteen, Gina felt a little embarrassed at her own continuing interest in hanging out with a warrior clan kid. She was already considered strange enough at school. She was one of the few mixed-race kids in her class. Her darker skin tone stood out and standing out was seldom a good thing in school. She had already started to think about moving to Kanera for university. A Tokarei city to the south, Kanera, had a more diverse population, where Gina would be able to go unnoticed

Another new hobby of hers was visiting the weekly Djanian market in Grantan. Since her friendships at school were superficial at best, she had a lot of free time on the weekends. She started to look forward to the market and spend hours combing their stalls. She also liked that, among breesians, she was just another human, not Raninali, not Tokari, just Gina. She liked the anonymity.

She had seen many carpets and woven tapestries. The textures and colours enchanted her. But they were always far too expensive for her to purchase. She had started to try to memorise some of the Djanian greetings and called out to the stall owners that she visited regularly.

In a particular stall, she found a thin woven band that looked like it might have once been a necklace. She found the complexity of the design beautiful, and she picked it up and without thinking, started wrapping it around her wrist, like a bracelet. The breesian behind the stall was watching her curiously.

"What ingenuity you have!" the shopkeeper called to her in Nülandish.

Gina jumped, not realising she'd been observed, "Oh... well ... It's such a pretty design. Was it once a necklace?"

"It was! It had broken, and I had thought to repair it, but somehow it must've ended up in my stall. I think you have a wonderful way of improvising! With our gauntlets, we can never wear this jewellery as bracelets. You have given this necklace new life. Allow me to see if I can close it with the traditional knot."

"W-Wait, I don't know if I can afford it," Gina protested, removing the bracelet.

"I can offer you a good price." The breesian said, his gauntleted hands gently picking up the ends of the necklace-turned-bracelet. With impressive dexterity, he tied the ends in an elegant, complex bow, and said the price softly as he did so.

Gina's eyes opened wide. The price was ridiculously low. She could afford it! She nodded her head and when the bracelet was tied securely on her wrist, she reached into her bag to pull out the cash to pay the shopkeeper.

She admired her wrist on her way home.

41

Mendani, Hunter

Vraya was shocked by Hunter's speed. She jumped back making space between her and Hunter. Rowan was relieved to see Hunter had joined the fight.

Vraya commanded all her drones to attack Hunter. But nothing happened. She looked around and saw that the remaining drones had already been sliced to pieces. Hunter stood ready to cut Vraya down. Vraya got in position to shred Hunter to pieces. The two looked at each other with dead eyes. They were about to charge at each other when Rowan fell to the ground, unconscious. Hunter noticed and went to Rowan. Vraya made a run for it, she knew when she was in a fight she can't win.

Rowan was bleeding heavily after the fight with Vraya. He was deeply wounded in several places. Hunter didn't know what to do. Hunter carried Rowan on his back, looking for a doctor. But, in the breesian area, it wasn't easy for humans to find a doctor. They walked for a few streets, but Rowan couldn't stay conscious anymore, he was losing too much blood.

"He's going to die if you don't treat his wounds quickly," said a voice.

Hunter recognized the voice. He looked behind him, it was Vraya.

"What do you want?"

"Nothing. I'm here to help you, let me take care of him."

"How can I trust you?"

"I'm a doctor. And right now, you don't have a choice."

Hunter decided to trust Vraya with Rowan. Hunter carried Rowan to Vraya's home. She opened her door and went to prepare for the surgery. Hunter went inside with caution; it could still be a trap. Even so, he placed Rowan on the operating table and saw Vraya exchange her battle gauntlets for a medical pair. Rowan's fate was now in Vraya's hands.

Hunter explored her house as he waited for the operation to be finished. He found Vraya's workshop, it was a massive space. In one corner, he could see her work on different types of drones. Before today, he'd never seen a drone before, though they had been mentioned in some of his grandpa's old warrior history books. Warrior clans knew that on Thaedim, tech and magic had been fused into small flying machines that had attacked alongside the demons. A magic-based power source was fused onto a metal form that could be manipulated for any purpose from spying to bombing.

In Djania, this fusing of magic and techology was strictly forbidden. Hundreds of years ago, when breesians that showed a talent for magic had been expelled from Djania and forced to live on Thaedim, they began to combine magic with technology. Their experiments had caught the attention of the Djanian government. It was the reason that the Djanians had first gone to war with Thaedim.

Hunter had never imagined such a variety of drones. In Vraya's workshop he saw medical drones next to delivery drones, and every type of battle drone scattered about the room. They were all waiting for the power source to be fused to the metal frame and motor. Hunter remembered Gina talking about how Djanians hated magic. Well, he thought to himself, here was a Djanian that had fused tech and magic, Vraya was something special.

He moved on from the drone area. In another part of the workspace, it seemed that she was working on a motor vehicle. He could have sworn he saw designs for single-passenger personal airships as well. She was clearly a genius.

Two long hours later, all the bullets were removed. Vraya came out of the operating room, while Rowan slept off the sedatives. He would need some weeks to heal. She found Hunter in her workshop

"This isn't the waiting area." Vraya said, narrowing her eyes at Hunter.

"Vraya," Hunter said, looking straight at her, "will you join us?"

42

Prancinia, Gina

Gina, Brtann and Rngal went into the conference room, it had also been designed with the comfort of both humans and Djanians in mind. Gina looked across the long table. It was not just Montel. Gina had expected a check in on her assignment, an informal discussion and maybe to talk through the incident with Nkano.

Next to Montel were several Djanians, a few wearing the regalia associated with the Djanian government. They were flanked by translators and, Gina noticed, security guards.

Both Rngal and Brtann froze when they saw the other Djanians. Brtann began to react, almost lunging for the door. But he stopped when he realised it would leave Rngal and Gina, and there was no way he could get out of the building without being caught.

Instead, he calmly walked to a seat close to Gina, he felt protective of her and didn't want to get her tangled up with his past. Rngal followed.

The doors closed behind them, and the meeting began.

"Gina" Montel began, "so nice to see you again. How are you?"

"Montel, hello. It's nice to see you again too," Gina said tentatively. The last time they met, it had ended on decidedly chilly footing, so she didn't understand where this friendly tone was coming from. She continued, “I'm doing well. It's my first time in Prancinia. It's an amazing place.” She placed her hands on the table and clasped them nervously in front of her. Everyone in the room noticed her bracelet, and also her bandaged wrist.

“Yes, I spend a few months here each year. It’s different every time. It’s truly impressive,” Montel said, directing the compliment to his Djanian companions on his side of the table. Each time they spoke, the interpreters were communicating what was being said. Gina grew more nervous. “But what’s this?” Montel asked, gesturing to her bandage.

“Oh uh…” Gina began but hesitated as she wasn’t sure if she should explain the whole story in front of the other visitors.

Montel seemed to come to the same conclusion and rescued her: “Never mind, we can talk about that later.”

She could sense that both Brtann and Rngal were on edge. Neither of them had spoken yet, and she knew Brtann was a master diplomat, skilled at putting everyone at ease. Somehow his powers of persuasion were negated.

Gina fidgeted in her chair.

“So -uh- Montel, what is this about?” She glanced over at the officials I haven’t heard anything about how I’ve been doing my job.” Gina ventured, hoping to understand what was going on, she wondered if it was about the attack from Nkano. The government officials had yet to be introduced.

When Gina first met Montel months ago during her interview process, she was wrong-footed. It was still odd for her to look at someone that seemed to be her own age but was clearly in behaviour and mannerisms much older and higher than her status-wise in their company. When she'd encountered him during the Denma training, she'd said the wrong thing. But after reading his book, she felt she had some insights into who he was. She wondered if he knew how revealing that book was. She didn't want things to go wrong again, which is why she tried to cut to the chase now.

43

Prancinia, Brtann

Five years ago, the year 6098

After arriving in Djania, Brtann hid in Prancinia, using the small amount of cash the shop could spare. He wondered if the Liunian government might try to find him, even on Breeland.

He felt certain that Sunnico would be looking for him. He didn't know what Lnore ended up doing with the contract, but he feared that he might put her in danger if he tried to contact her.

He didn't know how much Danica knew of what was going on in the Raven District. She must be aware of the roll out of the gambling machines via their sub-brands, but did her connections go all the way to the drugs that were being pumped into the casinos? Was this another trial that Sunnico was carrying out? Or were they looking to addict an entire population to a drug that would soon come to market?

He had a few connections that he'd made in the years he'd been scouting the city for products to sell in his shop. He managed to reach out to his contacts one by one for a few months of work and a place to stay. Weeks turned into months, and he soon realised that nearly three years had passed, evading detection from anyone from his life in Redall. He was constantly afraid. None of his contacts were stable enough to offer him a more permanent solution.

Brtann had finally run out of options. His mind had gone to Rngal several times when he was desperate for a friend, but he'd hesitated because of her connection to Sunnico for as long as he'd had other options. Now, his only remaining chance was to find Rngal and see if she could help get him out of the city.

He knew where her office was and lurked outside for a few days. Although his colouring was uncommon, in a city full of breesians there were several others with grey fur, so he was not as eye-catching as when he lived in Redall, he dressed blandly, and hoped he did not stand out.

Finally, he saw Rngal emerging from the building.

He tracked her for a little while and just as she was going to board the light rail in the direction of the Sunnico tech hub. He reached out to bump his tail lightly into her. She stumbled a little, surprised at the contact.

"Brtann? This one hasn't seen you in years!"

Over the short time he'd known her, she'd quickly adapted to getting right to the point. Though she still had the itching sensation that she was being rude when she did so.

"I know -ah- this one has been here. How are things at Sunnico?"

She pulled him aside and that's when he saw her gauntlets, they were a prototype that he'd seen on Lnore's workbench. So Lnore had gone through with the contract, and it seemed that Rngal was Sunnico's tester for the functionality of the product.

Brtann had taken a few pairs of gauntlets with him, but almost exclusively wore Lnore's latest version. He kept his fists closed, to hide the vicious claws.

He could tell from her body language that she was hesitant to trust him.

“This one finds it to be progressing smoothly.” When she returned to the formal speech, Brtann knew he needed to figure out a way to get her to trust him, because, for now, she saw him with suspicion.

“This one would appreciate a chance to speak further.” He said tentatively, his ears turning towards her hopefully.

“This one concurs. But not now. This one will meet you here tomorrow at sunset.”

“I’ll be there.” Brtann broke the formal speech patterns in his eagerness to confirm the meeting.

44

Prancinia, Montel

Montel considered Gina's question. He was not quite ready to move on to the next step of the meeting, which was far from routine. He was now concerned for Gina's safety, seeing that she was injured, and had noted her new bracelet. He wanted to find out if she had managed to uncover more about Rominore in her short time in Ypare.

Montel tended to prefer staying out of the spotlight. Gina's guess had been right all those months ago: his mother had been a warrior from the Wanyd clan in Emaich. His father had been an elf from Thaedim. In the early aftermath of the war, there were many displaced people trying to get away before the travel ban was enforced. Montel's father had not been permitted to leave the island, but his parents had worried about raising a half-human on a demon continent. So, his mother had returned, pregnant, to Emaich, just after the borders closed. She'd travelled back via an obscure sea route and landed on a quiet beach. Her return became lore among warrior clans, and soon became the template for how clan members could reach Thaedim to complete their training.

Upon returning, Montel's mother had renounced her warrior ways and tried to fit into society. When Montel was born, it was not immediately clear that he was half-Thaedish. His mother had hidden him until he had to go to school. The school administrators had reported him to the city authorities, and his mother had been called in to explain.

She had insisted that Montel was her child, born on Nüland soil, he was Emaichian by blood and birth. The city officials were dubious about the logic but had allowed Montel to go to school with the other children. From an early age his mother had insisted that he wear his hair long, covering his tell-tale ears. He fought it for a while, convinced it made his already gender-neutral looks even more ambiguous. But eventually he settled into the look and kept it now, many years after his mother had passed away. He was not yet middle-aged for an elf, and since he knew little about his father, he could only guess that he might live half of the typical elven lifespan of 400 years.

He had never trained in the warrior ways and only reluctantly acknowledged his in-born talents. He had no interest in discovering what power he may have inherited from his father, or if there was a chance to be Awakened on a training mission to Thaedim. He was a product of the war and wanted nothing to do with it. Instead, he had followed a human path to success, getting a job at Denma almost 50 years ago now.

When he'd joined Denma he'd hidden what he was for years, but eventually it had been necessary to explain why he wasn't ageing to a few trustworthy colleagues. They had already seen his promise and when they realised his potential to steer the company in the long term, they had brought him into upper management. About 25 years ago he had begun the outreach to Djania, believing it to be an opportunity to again bridge these cultures that were drifting apart in peacetime.

Breesians had a longer lifespan than humans and a longer memory. They could tell what he was, and it had taken him nearly a decade to convince those in power in Djania that he, although half-Thaedian, was not a threat. But he had time, he studied, wrote several books on their culture. He had also built up Denma's business interests. The architecture of Denma's headquarters in

Prancinia was his own folly, and he regretted it every time he looked at it. Such a foolish choice, but it was done now and the Djanians had accepted it, eventually.

Back in the present, Montel shifted in his seat, as if he'd just remembered the point of the meeting, "Right, right, good that you asked that. First off, let me say that we are very pleased with the progress you are making. The reports are excellent. Also from your supervisors," he said, nodding towards Brtann and Rngal. It was the first time he'd acknowledged them.

All three of the new arrivals remained on edge, waiting for his next words.

"However, there is—ahem—a new request that we've been asked to consider." Montel gestured to the Djanians sitting next to him.

Finally, given their cue, the government officials stood, as was traditional for Djanians.

"On behalf of the culture ministry, there is a request that the experiment in Ypare is stopped," the first one said.

The second one said, "The participants in this experiment are needed elsewhere."

45

Mendani, Hunter

"What do you mean?" Vraya asked with suspicion.

Even though it was her house, Hunter gestured for her to sit, and they sat across from each other in her workshop.

Hunter looked at Vraya and asked, "Why did you help us? There was no reason for it. Why would you help an enemy?"

"I already told you, I just wanted to help."

"I don't buy it; there must have been something in it for you."

Vraya stayed silent.

"I looked around your house, I saw some of your projects. I know you're not just some doctor moonlighting as a pickpocket. You're a genius."

Vraya sighed, "Fine, I guess you're not just brawn after all. I helped your friend because I want to go to the Eternal Garden. And I know that's also your goal."

"Wait, how do you know that?"

"You guys talk really loud, you know."

"Ok." Hunter said, making a mental note to speak more guardedly when he could be overheard. Somewhere in the back of his mind, he could feel his grandpa yelling at him for being so careless.

Vraya continued, "And I attacked you to see if you're strong enough to make it to the Eternal Garden. Nobody is getting to the centre of Thaedim unless they are Tyrants or stronger. A Tyrant alone has no chance. But with you and your friend, we might just have a chance. I think you're the first Destroyer I've met." She stopped for a second and she almost looked guilty, "And I took your money to get you to fight me." As she said that, she reached into her pocket and tossed the money pouches at Hunter, who caught them without effort.

"Awakened." Hunter corrected as he slid the pouches into his backpack. Vraya sat back, looking at him with surprise.

"Definitely the first Awakened I've met."

"So, what you're saying is that you want to join me."

"Not join you, I want a truce, an alliance."

"An alliance, sure, you can join us, we may need to work on Rowan a bit though."

"Well, thank you, but I am not joining you. This is just temporary."

Hunter shrugged. A few hours later, he was looking for a place to sleep. He found a hotel not far from Vraya's house. He stayed there for the next few nights. Rowan stayed in Vraya's surgery, there were rooms for patient recovery.

Since they had to wait until Rowan was sufficiently healed before they could leave Mendani, they both needed to find ways to fill the days. For Vraya, it wasn't hard, she had her workshop and drones to rebuild after the fight with Rowan.

Meanwhile Hunter had a lot of free time in his hands. He tried to explore

Mendani, but the city wasn't very large and in just a few hours he had already seen everything. Hunter was bored and he didn't have motivation to do anything. But then he spotted a young dwarf boy practising with an axe. That reminded Hunter of when he was young. That little boy gave him motivation to train. For the next few weeks, Hunter trained. He trained his concentration, his strength, his speed, and his agility. He was hoping to gain some control over the powers he knew were Awakening, but he couldn't bring it back.

When Rowan woke up, Hunter visited him often, and soon enough, he was almost healed from his wounds. Hunter was happy to see Rowan awake again. They told Rowan the news of Vraya coming with them to the Eternal Garden. It took him a moment to accept it, but once he heard how she had saved his life, he knew it was the right decision.

After that, they got ready to leave the city. They were eager to see what lay ahead, although they knew that the most dangerous part was yet to come. Only native Thaedians lived further inland than Mendani. They left the city and headed for the Eternal Garden.

46

Prancinia, Montel

According to his instructions, Montel directed his next question to the officials "Now friends, who is needed where?" He was quietly certain that no one cared where Gina went. He was especially certain that he would not allow her to end up with either group. He fully intended for her to come back to Nüland. She would go back with him.

A vivid discussion broke out among the Djanians. Montel, who had seen these Djanian debates last many hours before, stood and crossed the table to stand next to Gina. He held his hand out to her. "We can get out of here, Denma Corp is out of it," he said softly, leaning forward and motioning his head towards the door.

Gina stood but refused Montel's hand. She'd started to appreciate her time in Ypare, Rngal and Brtann had become real friends. Nkano was scary, but they would handle him together. She was certain that this project was being carried out, uninterrupted, in small towns throughout Djania. Why was her project being stopped?

She thought about Hunter, despite his power, he seemed to be carried along by life.

She wanted to stop what was happening, she closed her eyes, focused her mind, and wondered if this is what it took to be Awakened. But no. She couldn't access clan magic; she had nothing that could protect Brtann or Rngal.

As she looked again around the room, she saw that the officials had decided who was going where. Brtann going in one direction, Rngal going in the other. Both showed no resistance.

"Wait" Gina called out in Djanian. "This one does not want to be separated and calls on the soul of Breeland, who has protected its children for thousands of years and will go on to safeguard them ever more, to fortify and protect this phana bond." She had initiated the ancient phana bond.

The room froze. Gina had memorised the phana invocation from Montel's book and was using it now, not knowing if there was any chance of success for a human to invoke the magic of Breeland. She looked up hopefully, in the direction of Rngal and Brtann.

Rngal replied: "This one would remain within the phana bond and calls on the heart of Breeland, who has nurtured its children for thousands of years and will go on to ensure their future ever more."

The air seemed to shimmer for a fraction of a second as the world readjusted. It was done.

A human had bonded herself to a Djanian with the phana. Nobody in the room knew what to do, none of them had any experience with the phana, but by Djanian tradition, they had to let the two go together. Gina slipped away from Montel's side to Rngal's, following her out of the room. She became aware of a new mental bond that allowed her to share feelings and, maybe one day, full thoughts with Rngal.

Montel watched with equal parts awe and frustration as Gina left the room.

47

Prancinia, Brtann

Two years ago, the year 6101

At the agreed meeting point, Brtann waited for Rngal. Sure enough, she arrived and invited him to a lively cafe where they wouldn't be noticed.

They found a table with two couches, Rngal reclined against the one, Brtann took the other, but did not relax. He noted that the cafe was loud enough that it would be difficult to overhear their conversation.

"Nice gauntlets" he said, noticing she was still wearing the prototypes.

"Yes," she said almost purring, "these gauntlets are a game changer. My hands used to ache from my old pair, and they were top-of-the-line, provided by Sunnico. This is an amazing invention. Lnore is truly brilliant."

Brtann's heart convulsed; he missed Lnore terribly and had not been this long without her since they'd met all those years ago.

"However, implementation has been slower than the higher-ups would like, because she refuses to come onsite, perhaps you can convince her?"

Brtann felt a wave of shock, Rngal didn't know. She didn't know he was a murderer. He'd always trusted her, and they'd had a good rapport before, so he decided to trust her now.

“I don’t think that will happen. You see -ah- I’m out of the deal. Lnore is working on her own.”

Rngal said nothing but Brtann could tell with the slight shift in her posture, this news had surprised her. She was no longer reclining effortlessly, she now looked poised to flee if necessary.

“I don't want to go into the details, but I do need to tell you about what Sunnico is doing in Redall, in my home, the Raven District. They have taken it over with their gambling tech and Sunnico pharma is drugging the gamblers. You can't trust them.”

Rngal’s ears twitched. His story was lining up with a few conversations she’d been involved in when she’d been Danica’s full-time interpreter.

“I think…” She started, but then faltered, Rngal tried again, “I think I knew that.” She said, accepting the truth.

“I need to get out of the city, too many people from Sunnico know me here. Do you have any connections?”

Rngal thought quickly. “You’re not going to like it, but what about Ypare?”

PART 6 - NOW

Interlude 5

Hunter was sixteen, he had continued in his combat training. Neil was getting older and could no longer spar with him. Hunter had gotten used to the short blade and moved as if it was an extension of his body.

Neil decided it was time for Hunter to receive a new blade forged by the Veronn clan. Hunter's strength and adaptability was growing day by day. He had learned every fighting move there was to teach and was even coming up with his own original innovations. Neil commanded that the forges create a Sanalia blade for Hunter. Sanalia blades were only given to the most skilled Veronn clan warriors. There had not been a warrior with the talent to wield a Sanalia sword since Neil's brother, Markus, now long dead.

Neil decided to try to teach Hunter a few techniques that were reserved for clan members that were Awakened. They shouldn't work for just any clan member. The first technique was to control flames. He would take Hunter into the forges and get him to attempt to control the flames burning there. Although Hunter showed more concentration than when he was in the classroom, he never managed to master the lesson. Neil also introduced the mental techniques that could help an Awakened to control the flames that they had created. Teaching Hunter how to calm his mind and focus on putting out the flames.

Neil regretted that his brother never got to see the hopeful future for the clan that he could see in Hunter.

Sanalia swords were longer and narrower than the usual Veronn swords. It stood half as tall as Hunter. He asked Talik to create special embellishment for the blade's grip, so that it would form to Hunter's hand.

After weeks of work, the Sanalia blade emerged from the forges. It was perfect.

Neil gathered the remaining Veronn clan members for the ceremony that would initiate Hunter as a full clan member. Only training in Thaedim would make him a warrior. But this ceremony made him one of the Veronn clan.

Hunter treated the ceremony lightly. He did not see the value in these traditions, the same way he couldn't wrap his head around the clan history that Neil had been trying to teach him for nearly a decade.

Neil, knowing Hunter, curtailed the ceremony. In a short movement he presented the sword. That got Hunter's attention. He was hypnotised.

He reached for the Sanalia blade and the first time he touched it, he could feel its magic seeping into him. This blade was home. He backed away from his family, far enough so he could feel the heft and swing the sword. He felt the energy and power thrum through his arm. He swung the blade, cutting the air.

"This will do nicely," Hunter said with a grin.

48

Thaedim, Hunter

Hunter, Rowan and now Vraya had been walking for days since leaving Mendani.

"I'm getting tired of walking," said Hunter, grumpily.

"Don't worry, we'll reach the mountains soon, if you're tired of walking maybe some mountain climbing is what you need," said Vraya, sarcastically.

Hunter looked at Vraya, "Vraya I've been wondering, are you smaller than the average Djanian?"

"Yeah, so what?" Vraya answered, annoyed.

"Nothing, it's just that you're different from the other Djanians I've known."

Vraya didn't reply. She wanted to say that she wasn't Djanian. Her family had come from Rominore, but since she was a third generation breesian born on Thaedim, she wasn't sure she could claim any of that heritage.

"Knock it off Hunter, you shouldn't ask people questions they don't want to answer," said Rowan.

"Okay, Okay, maybe let's try something else. Rowan and me, we need to get to the Eternal Garden to finish our training, why do you need to go there?"

“Hunter…” Rowan started to tell his friend to shut up, but Vraya interrupted him.

“The herbs. The one you call benthe, is extremely powerful, and it is one reason. But not just that, I want to see if the rumours of a power source plant are true. If I could get one of those and find a way to make it grow at my house in Mendani, you have no idea what I could build.”

Hunter smiled, after visiting her workshop, he had several ideas of what she might create, given an unlimited magical power source.

They stopped talking, Hunter looked in front of him and saw from the distance some people walking. The travellers seemed to be walking from the opposite direction, so they would be passing each other in the next hour. The travellers drew closer, and Hunter could now see them clearer. Hunter noticed they were elves, he looked at Rowan and Vraya and sensed fear from both of them. When they passed each other, Hunter could feel how strong the elves were. Oddly, the elves left the foreigners alone.

When the elves were out of sight, Hunter asked: “Why were you guys so scared?”

“They were elves, it's only natural to be scared,” said Rowan.

“Remind me why that is.” Hunter said.

“You don’t know?” said Vraya.

Hunter shrugged.

“Elves were the force behind the Thaedim War. They live longer than us breesians and much longer than you humans. They were the reason the war went on so long. They kept us jumping through their hoops for hundreds of years. They’re also one of the races that rule this island, don’t underestimate them. That’s why I stay in Mendani: elves have mostly given up the outer cities.” said Vraya.

"Seriously, Hunter, nothing?" Rowan asked, clearly Vraya's description aligned with his understanding.

"Well, uh, forewarned is forearmed?" said Hunter, trying to meet them halfway.

"What is the Veronn clan education…?" Rowan said, unwisely

"You want to test me?" Hunter asked, his eyes going fiery.

"No, not me." said Rowan, backing down quickly.

As a distraction, Vraya cut in: "Just so both of you know, the centre of Thaedim is where the elves live now. They've given up the coast and cities like Killgaris, Mendani. I was surprised to see some of them coming our way. I wonder what their mission was. Maybe it's you." Vraya said, looking at Hunter.

"So… elves are some of the most dangerous demons." said Hunter.

"Yeah..." said Rowan, making an effort not to roll his eyes.

49

Prancinia, Rngal

Rngal had surprised herself by accepting the phana with Gina.

She looked over her shoulder to Brtann, he seemed to be in a daze. She wondered if he'd noticed what was happening.

Rngal and Gina were taken together to a new, smaller meeting room. The Djanian guards did not seem to know what to do now that there was a human involved. They were also out of their depth with the phana.

They hovered awkwardly around Gina and Rngal.

Rngal had no idea that Gina had studied Djanian culture enough to know that there was still magic in Djania. Let alone that one powerful, ancient spell could make the very land shift around you. She could feel Gina's presence lightly in the corners of her thoughts. Rather than intrusive, it felt comforting. All would be well if they stayed together.

Gina's passion for Djania mirrored Rngal's own interest in all things human. Rngal had never heard of the phana being invoked by a non-breesian and had not thought it was possible. Evidently it was. She wondered if her species' magic might have been embracing Gina and her wholehearted commitment to Breeland.

They stood together, with the government official and a security guard, for a short while.

Then the door opened, and a Djanian indicated that it was time to leave. They exited the building, and two vehicles appeared. The official got into one. The security guard ushered Gina and Rngal into the other. Rngal noticed the Sunnico logo on the car's door.

As the scenery sped by, Rngal realised where they were going. To Sunnico's tech hub in Prancinia. Rngal's old workplace. When she'd returned to Ypare a year ago, Rngal had wanted to make up for having inadvertently facilitated Sunnico's interests. She wanted to remove her talents and slow their progress long enough so that she could figure out a plan with Brtann on how to stop them. She'd thought the government contract would shield them for longer. She could only think that Sunnico had somehow bribed the government and manipulated Montel at the same time.

The transfer felt like it had only taken moments. Rngal arrived with chagrin. The last time she left the tech hub, she'd intended never to see it again. When she checked the mental bridge to Gina, she could tell the human was overwhelmed.

Well, Rngal thought to herself, why shouldn't she be? She'd just spent the last months cooped up in a small town. And then a day in Prancinia only to end up virtually a prisoner at Sunnico and connected by the phana for life.

They arrived and were escorted into a meeting area.

The security guard waited until another Djanian came into the room. "Krenn!" Rngal burst out before she could think.

"Rngal." He replied.

"Wh-what's going on?"

"I think that's what we'd like to ask you. When you disappeared a year ago, we figured you'd go to your hometown, but we were surprised to see that you'd caught up with Brtann. We've been watching you two for a while now. And what's this?" Krenn's ears flicked towards Gina. He seemed to squint for a moment, "The phana? Really? That's dramatic, even for you."

"I'm surprised you can tell."

"It's not that hard. But don't think that this is going to mean anything to Danica."

"We are still in Djania, she cannot control everything."

"Perhaps. Well, no matter, one human won't make a difference."

"We want you back and we want our prototypes. You can take those off now."

Rngal raised her arms. Krenn flicked a switch to release the gauntlets that Rngal had on. He gestured to the wall, where numerous gaunlets rested in wall mounts "Choose another pair. These," he indicated the pair Rngal had been wearing, "belong to Sunnico." He carried the Rngal's gauntlets into another room.

She put on a replacement pair of gauntlets. After years of wearing Lnore's gauntlets, she felt the heaviness of the new gauntlets as she flexed her fingers, she could tell that this new pair was stiff and awkward to use.

Krenn returned and said: "We have set up your accommodation here. You will not leave. We will find a room for your pet."

Gina stiffened but said nothing. Rngal could feel that Gina was beginning to wonder if going with Montel back to Denma and just getting slotted into another town might've been the better option.

Rngal had not been surprised that Sunnico had found them. She knew that

Ypare was hardly an original idea for a hiding place and that she and Brtann could be found at any moment, if Sunnico cared enough. The true level of what Sunnico was doing was a secret, even to the Djanian government.

Apparently Brtann leaving on his own was not enough, it must've been the two of them deserting that had gotten Danica's attention.

She had been surprised that Sunnico had managed to break the government contract with Denma. It was only when that contract had been secured between Denma and the local government of Ypare that Rngal had felt able to make her own move away from Sunnico, that this programme would offer a way out.

But now it seemed she'd just dragged Gina into the Sunnico mess. Part of her was at least grateful that her family and hometown had been spared from the worst of the spectacle.

50

Prancinia, Brtann

The government official and security guard escorted Brtann out of the meeting room from the opposite side from where Rngal and Gina had gone. They took him directly out of the building, where a vehicle with a Sunnico logo was waiting. He slumped further; he was caught, after all. Unlike Rngal and Gina, Brtann was taken to a hotel near the airship docking station and into a hotel room with the security guard keeping a close eye on his captive. After about an hour, the security guard left.

Shortly after, the door opened. "Brtann, I'm so glad we've found you. I have to say you left us in quite a lurch when you disappeared."

"Danica" Brtann's ears were flattened back and his tail flashed outwards, making him seem larger, looming over her. It was just the two of them in the room. Brtann's gauntlets flashed as he moved, pinning Danica to the wall.

"Now, now, I hope you know that I don't agree with violence. Like you, I prefer persuasion."

"Persuade me." He snarled; his grip tightened.

"We're going to Redall. I think you'll be interested to see how Lnore has fared these last five years."

Brtann's arms dropped, and he stood back. Danica righted herself, rubbing her arms where his grip would no doubt leave bruises. She was right, he could not follow through with the attack. She'd mentioned that she could bring him back to his wife, to his home. He wondered how she could get him back into Liunia without consequences. Sunnico was a powerful company, but he hadn't imagined it was above the law.

"You really should be more careful with those," Danica gestured to his gauntlets, "You might have an accident one day," she said viciously, and then continued in a business-like manner "We're boarding an airship to Liunia tomorrow. If you need to bring anything, the time to tell me is now."

He considered his options. He could try to escape, but where would that lead? His home in Ypare would no doubt be barred from him. His contacts in Prancinia had been exhausted. Denma only knew him via the government and had already made a deal with Sunnico to hand him over. He wondered what Sunnico had offered them. He wanted to go back to Redall, but to go back as Danica's puppet was unbearable. If he went back on his own, the authorities would surely find him.

There wasn't any option that made sense. He flexed his fingers inside the gauntlet as he made up his mind.

"I have everything that I need."

"Good."

"But one thing Danica."

"Hmm?" She had already lost interest now that the struggle was over.

"Rngal, Gina. What will happen to them? If I agree to this, you must ensure that they are not harmed."

"Rngal is extremely valuable to us. Have no fear for her. Charming how you think you are the only prize we were after." Danica laughed without humour. "Who's Gina?"

"Rngal's companion."

"Ah, that shouldn't be a problem. She's human? I think we can find something for her to do." Danica dismissed the subject.

Brtann spent an uncomfortable night in the hotel room alone, a guard just outside his door. He did not sleep.

51

Prancinia, Montel

Montel had returned to his office after the encounter with Gina, Brtann and Rngal. The meeting room was now empty after the commotion of just an hour ago.

He'd let it happen. He'd been designated the representative of Denma to Djania and he'd lost to Sunnico.

Denma and Sunnico were not direct rivals, but they certainly swam in the same pool. As the two largest human companies, they were the only ones with significant outposts in Prancinia. Making their mark on Djania, they could not afford to be seen as in opposition to each other, so they played nice in the Djanian capital. On Nüland, they made it a point not to interact. Denma offered services, Sunnico offered products. There was little chance for overlap, but by virtue of being the only notable human companies in Breeland, the two had to make an effort to represent human culture positively.

It had been years ago when Montel had first thought of the cultural exchange that would be facilitated by Denma. He'd been watching as a new political group had taken control of Prancinia. They'd had an outward-looking mindset. They wanted to exploit the airships that were beginning to be an important connection between Djania and Nüland.

Airships had been developed in Djania as bombers during the war. The engines and flying mechanism were pure Djanian inventions. In peacetime, they had been converted into passenger vessels. Djania had imported Rominore designers and human engineers to design the passenger area. The first airships had been slow, unreliable, and uncomfortable. But they had become an essential tool. The airships connected Breeland and Nüland, via a direct route. By taking the highest altitudes, they could fly directly over Thaedim without having to engage with demons.

Previously, the only way to cross between the continents had been by sea. Which had meant either circumventing the island with a wide berth or trying to race past it not far from the coast. It had been perilous to cross and took weeks at best. Airships had reduced the travel time to just 3 days.

For the last 30 years the airships had connected the two continents and allowed for a renewal of cooperation and collaboration between humans and breesians. The new Djanian government wanted to expand and exploit this partnership. One of the first steps to that end was getting their population accustomed to the human ways, while also endearing the humans to Djania.

Montel's proposal to embed young, mostly good-looking, enthusiastic humans into Djanian outposts had first sounded ridiculous to Denma Corp management. But they'd let him explore it with his contacts. It had taken years, but he had nothing but time.

Nearly ten years of laying the groundwork was followed by two years of negotiating and another two years of preparations, including the recruitment of the new Denma employees. The Djanian government recruited Djanians with sufficient language and cultural abilities that could be placed in local town halls to direct the project. Montel had not met every one of the 250 new hires; he'd only joined for the interviews of candidates that showed promise as long-term collaborators in this project. This is how he'd first encountered Gina. With her extensive studies in Djanian history as well as culture and good grasp of the language and customs, she was possibly well suited to take over the project, once the pilot phase had been completed.

Having her experience the exchange first-hand meant that she would understand how it could be adapted and possibly improved in the future. This was why they had chosen a particularly rural and uneventful placement for her, to give her a gentle launch onto this career path. Montel was concerned that she'd injured her wrist, so perhaps it had not been such a safe choice after all.

Instead of having his future project manager here and promoted early to her protégé role, she was now in the hands of Sunnico according to ancient Breeland magic.

He hadn't yet let himself think about how Gina had invoked the phana. It was beyond anything that he could have fathomed from his studies all those years ago. It seemed that *she* was the one teaching him about how Breeland worked now.

Montel called an assistant into the room. "Get me Karla, we have a situation."

Karla was another vice-president of Denma, and a workaholic. Within about an hour, she appeared on a screen before him.

"Montel," she said coldly, "To what do I owe this pleasure?"

"We've had a breach. It's Sunnico. They used government contacts to interrupt one of the pilot experiments and took one of our highly capable recruits as well."

He continued, "I don't think we can do anything about the Djanian government employees, but we must get Gina back. You remember, she was our best option for the growth and continuation of this project."

Karla winced. Dealings with Sunnico were always delicate. She did not want an all-out conflict with the other company, and she did not like some skirmish in Prancinia being the cause of it. But she was also aware of what Montel's project meant for Denma in Prancinia, they were taking over as the dominant human company, the most recognizable to Djanians. Achieving this would open doors to more government contracts and also connections to Djania's own corporations.

"How did it happen?" She asked.

"Two government officials came to me asking that Gina's pilot be ended early because the Djanian team was needed elsewhere and there were no other Djanians suitable for the pilot in Ypare. It was understood that Gina would return to us and begin her training early, considering the promising educational background and good early performance reviews we'd been getting from Ypare. She was ready for the next phase. Everything was going smoothly, until inexplicably, Gina invoked something called the phana. It is a Djanian kind of magic…"

"Magic? In Djania?" Karla cut in.

"It's obscure, but yes, there is some magic here. And they are required to respect it and it bonded her to one of the Djanians from Ypare, who we'd already agreed to hand over to the authorities. It was only as they were leaving that I saw that they were getting into Sunnico vehicles."

He grimaced and continued, "I can only think that Sunnico bribed the government to get access to the Djanians. As far as I can tell, they don't seem interested in Gina. Although," Montel mused out loud, "if Sunnico finds these Djanians of such interest, perhaps we should learn more about them. Let me do some research, I can get you more information."

Karla massaged her temples, already anticipating the headache this situation would cause. "All right Montel, we'll look into it." She disappeared from the screen.

Montel leaned back from his desk, for now, he would have to wait until he heard back from Karla. He called in another assistant. "Get me the names and backgrounds of the Djanians in Ypare. Anything you can find, and I want you to dig deep. Last ten years, at least."

52

Prancinia, Gina

Gina was amazed that her gamble had paid off.

Rngal was more traditionally breesian than Brtann, but Gina had also bonded with her in Ypare. Gina wasn't sure why the phana had worked for her, but she had studied Djania earnestly, with the intent to understand breesians. This had affected Rngal, and it seemed to be why Rngal had reacted when Gina had invoked the phana.

Although she couldn't yet discern the jumble of emotions that were spilling over the new mental bond into clear thoughts, Gina could sense that Rngal worried that she'd gotten Gina tangled up in something worse.

Gina had been shown to one of the human quarters in the compound. She'd collapsed into it with relish. Although she slightly criticised herself for this reaction. Hadn't she just lived comfortably for months in Ypare?

But she had to confess that a room designed for humans made a difference, no matter the comforts that Brtann had installed in her flat in Ypare. This room was standard issue for human visitors and designed for their every comfort. She luxuriated in it, even while she knew she was locked in.

The next morning the locks were lifted. Gina stepped out early, eager to find

Rngal and see what this tech hub had to offer. She had an open-air corridor with stairs to a giant courtyard in front of her room. Standing just outside her door, she watched the morning unfold.

One by one, as every morning, a series of metal doors opened. From one side hundreds of Djanian workers, without gauntlets, emerged from their sleep chambers. They moved as a group to a central depository of gauntlets. From there, they streamed into the factories on the far end of the courtyard.

Gina watched this sad progression. A handful of the Djanians acknowledged her. She didn't understand the signal.

Years later, she would understand that they had mistaken her for a visiting Sunnico scientist who required their respect.

53

Thaedim, Hunter

Hunter, Rowan and Vraya walked until they reached the base of a mountain range, The elves and other demons used the natural land barriers to protect their cities and the Eternal Garden. According to Hunter's map, climbing the mountain was the only option.

Rowan's natural affinity with the land made mountain climbing a friendly challenge, but he soon discovered that he had a fear of heights. Vraya easily climbed the mountain, her huge gauntlets gipping the rock with ease. Her drones stayed in a giant backpack.

Hunter wasn't struggling, thanks to his training while Rowan was injured, he'd gotten stronger than before. When they reached the top of the mountain, it almost seemed like they had reached heaven: they had a beautiful view of Thaedim.

With his new and intense fear of heights Rowan refused to climb down, Vraya helped him by using her drones to help him climb down. The other side of the mountain was filled with elves and an elven city was just a short distance away from the base of the mountain. They were all aware of how dangerous this place was.

They reached the other side of the mountain and before long found a clearing to rest for a little while. Just as they caught their breath, five elves appeared. Hunter unsheathed his blade. Vraya released her drones. Rowan pulled his spear out. The elves had not yet reacted, the leader of the group started to speak.

An explosion grabbed their attention. It was far away, but something was hurtling in their direction.

"What the hell was that?" Rowan yelled.

Something came flying into the clearing, knocking over several massive trees as it crashed in between Hunter's group and the elves.. The smoke cleared from the body; it was a dragon, now half buried in dirt and tree roots.

The dragon was several times larger than the one that had tried to flay Hunter when he'd first arrived on Thaedim. It seemed several Classes more powerful too. Hunter was shocked to see a Destroyer Class dragon thrown through the forest like it was nothing. Hunter thought to himself that the only thing that could beat such a creature must be a Dominion. But it can't be, he reasoned, there are only six of them. What are the chances that one would show up?

As if in answer to Hunter's silent question, an elf was flying effortlessly towards the clearing. He alighted smoothly in the middle of the clearing, his eyes still focused on the dragon. The elf carried a dagger in each hand, he was tall with a huge scar on his chest and looked like he had spent several human lifetimes fighting. He was clearly a Dominion.

"We *had* agreed that dragons are no longer welcome on this side of the mountains, yet here you are..." he said in a disappointed voice to the dragon, who whimpered from beneath a tree trunk.

Hunter, Rowan and Vraya were struggling to breathe properly around the Dominion, his presence was overwhelming. Even the other elves were filled with fear. Rowan couldn't move. Everything in Vraya's body was telling her to run.

The Dominion made eye contact with Hunter. "Hmm, what's this?" he said, finally acknowledging the scene in front of him.

Hunter was ready to fight him. But there was an uneasy feeling that Hunter had never felt before. This was the strongest opponent he had ever faced. He looked at his hands and saw that they were shaking. He couldn't hold his sword properly. This was the first time Hunter has ever faced fear. The Dominion walked towards him and all he could do was struggle with his sword.

As the Dominion was closing in, Vraya's drones opened fire on him. Hunter was relieved, he'd forgotten that drones couldn't feel fear. Thanks to that moment of distraction, Hunter was wide awake. He stopped shaking and was ready to fight. He looked back and saw that Vraya's drones had been destroyed. Hunter knew he had to go all out to even try and win this fight, blue flames burst into the air around him and he got into position to strike.

The Dominion smiled and kept advancing, "I've seen that technique before."

PART 7 - CONVERGENCE

Interlude 6

“Check it out, Gina, a Sanalia sword! I've only ever heard about them, this is the first one I've actually seen. And grandpa had it made for me!”

As was their usual dynamic, whatever fascinated Hunter, baffled Gina and vice versa. She looked the sword over. It was pretty, but beyond that, she couldn't see what was so special about it.

“Yeah, it looks like it has some of your dad’s craftsmanship too, no?”

“You noticed!” Hunter said excitedly, mistaking her comment for interest. He started swinging the blade around.

“Watch it!” Gina yelped as the blade came a bit too close. But there was no way that Hunter would be so careless as to let the blade make contact. In the days since he’d received the sword, he had already bonded with it completely and wielded it like it was a weapon he’d trained with since childhood.

Even at eighteen, Gina had not made any close friends. Her sense of isolation from her peers had brought her closer to Hunter over the years. He was still an annoying kid most of the time, but as a fellow mixed-race person in Grantan, they had a lot in common and had become fast friends.

She had continued her informal study of the Djanian language. She was a regular at the markets now and would engage in informal conversations with the breesians there. About a year ago she had started thinking of continuing her studies in the Djanian language, history, and culture degree programme at

Kanera university. She had applied a few weeks ago.

She hadn't told Hunter her plan yet. Though he was well aware of her growing obsession with Djania.

Gina saw how thrilled he was with his sword and thought this might be an opportunity to break the news to him.

“I wanted to tell you something. I got accepted into Kanera University. The Djanian studies programme.”

“What?” Hunter asked, missing his footing from a complicated attack formation he’d started to practise.

“I got the letter last week. Once graduation is done, I’m moving to Kanera.” She said quickly, feeling guilty.

“Oh.” Hunter said, without much expression. But knowing Gina so well, he quickly followed up: “I’m happy for you. This is what you wanted.”

So, he did listen, after all.

Gina nodded, relieved that he could see that she was following her dream. “Yeah, and it’s not *that* far, I’ll be back for holidays.”

“Only if the Djanian markets are no good. If they’re any good, we’ll never see you again!” He teased.

Gina laughed.

54

Redall, Brtann

When morning came, and Brtann was let out of the hotel room by a Sunnico security guard. He had another urge to escape but dampened his instincts. He was brought to the airship docking station where Danica was waiting.

The security guards stayed behind in Djania.

A three-day journey by airship to get to Nüland, and then another half day from the coast to Redall.

Brtann remembered the last time he'd been on an airship; he'd been on the run. He never thought he'd return home.

Danica had left him alone for the majority of the trip. She'd booked the luxury class tickets for both of them. When Brtann had been travelling regularly between the two continents, he'd only been able to afford the cheapest tickets. It was strange and indulgent to experience what Danica no doubt took for granted each time she travelled.

As they approached the outskirts of Redall, Brtann tried to hide his trembling. He was so close to Lnore. But he was also a wanted criminal and now Danica's collaborator.

What would she demand next?

“I think we’ll go straight to Sunnico.” Danica said to their driver.

They arrived in the early afternoon. Brtann hesitated to step out into the sunlight. Would he be seen immediately? Was this an elaborate trap to get him back where the Redall authorities could arrest him? He couldn't fault them if they did. He was guilty, and nothing could change that.

When he crossed from the vehicle to the entrance of the building, his tail stretched along the side of the building, he making sure it was real.

Danica led the way in.

She did not let on what would happen next, so all he could do was follow her as her staff greeted her on their way in. A few called out surprised greetings to Brtann as well. They were Sunnico employees that he’d worked with over five years ago. He nodded his head, in the human manner, not trusting his voice.

They reached Danica’s office, and she closed the door. Finally, he would learn what she had in mind for him.

“Brtann, you look like shit. Did you get any sleep on the trip?”

“It wasn’t exactly a pleasure cruise for me.”

“Yes, yes, you've made that clear.” Danica looked exasperated. “We didn't go to the trouble - and not to mention expense - of getting you and Rngal out of your ridiculous hiding place, not to have a good reason to bring you here.”

“I can imagine.”

“I bet you have been. What have you come up with?”

“I don't know what your endgame is in the Raven District. But I know you need Lnore's gauntlets.” When he left Redall, he believed that Sunnico needed the deal with Lnore for her gauntlets so desperately that she would be safe. She could hold her own with the corporation. Or so he'd believed.

"True. And yet, we still have not managed to manufacture a single pair. This is what I need you for and why I've brought you back here. I need you to get Lnore to get on with the implementation with our engineers."

"Am I free?"

"Oh, *that*, yes, we took care of that days after you disappeared - it really was a waste that you held us back for these last few years just because a drug addict died in the street."

"A drug addict died in the street…" Brtann echoed. "That's not what happened- Sunnico- you were responsible!"

"Now, Brtann, that kind of thinking is unproductive." Danica cut him off. "And if we think carefully about it, you might recall that *you* were responsible. Sunnico has done you a favour. We've cleared your name so you can live here again with your wife. Now, in return, we need you to accelerate the gauntlet production. Can I count on you?"

It wasn't a question.

Brtann said nothing because there was nothing more to say.

"Meg!" Danica called sharply, "lead Brtann to the lab where Lnore is working on the gauntlets." she ordered. An assistant appeared and gestured for Brtann to follow, she seemed to be only a few years older than Gina.

As Brtann was walking out of Danica's office, another assistant walked in. "Danica, while you were away, we've had multiple calls from Denma. They're saying that we poached one of their newcomers to our tech hub. We haven't hired recently, so is this connected with…" The door slammed shut.

Brtann followed Meg through the hallways, from the corporate wing to the tech labs. Although much of the R&D took place at the tech hub in Djania, Danica had installed a small wing for tech innovations in Redall. She was keeping a close eye on all aspects of development. He wondered if she'd found new and even more devastating ways to deploy the drugs in the Raven District.

They reached a closed door.

"This is the room you want." Meg said and discreetly moved away. She had started working at Sunnico just a few months before Brtann had left for Djania and rememberd him from the early, optimistic days when he had first started negotiations with Sunnico. She knew Brtann had disappeared, but did not know why. She guessed that this was his first time seeing Lnore in many years. She was loyal to Sunnico, but interrupting this moment was not something she was willing to do. She disappeared back the way they had come from.

Brtann lingered in the hallway. He could not bring himself to open the door.

55

Prancinia, Montel

A week later, Montel was going over the extensive histories of Rngal and Brtann. "Well well, we may have something to negotiate with after all," he said to himself

He shared the bare minimum with Karla so that she could use it in the negotiations to get Gina back. Negotiations between two human companies that did not respect the phana.

Karla's request for access to Rngal and Brtann had been met with rejections. But she had discovered that Rngal and Gina had stayed in Djania, at the Sunnico tech hub, meanwhile Brtann had been taken to Redall, where Sunnico had its Nüland headquarters.

Although Montel rarely spent time in Liunia, he'd been to Redall a handful of times, many years ago and hadn't been impressed. When Sunnico set up their business in Redall, Montel had preferred to work for Denma, a more established company.

He had since had several encounters with Sunnico, and they had only confirmed in his mind that he had made the right choice. Over the many years that he'd worked for Denma, he'd helped guide it into the company it had become. The most recent news he'd heard out of Redall was that parts of the city were overrun with drug dealers.

Another few days and Montel received a call from Karla. "Montel, we've got Sunnico's green light to take Gina back."

Montel looked at Karla on the screen. "Do I want to know what we used as our bargaining chip?"

"Oh, they weren't interested in keeping Gina at Sunnico. They won't facilitate the separation with the Djanian, though. And, if you're right about the phana, it seems that might be a much bigger hurdle. So, Montel, over to you. We've done what we can, you need to do the rest." She cut the connection.

Montel knew that the phana was most frequently ended by the death of one of the participants. Montel did not want to resort to murder, especially now that he'd learned more about Rngal. It was unlikely that Sunnico would let her go. But if he could convince Gina to come with him, would the phana still bind them and would Rngal be obliged to join Denma? That would be a victory for Denma. But surely Sunnico would not let Rngal go.

56

Thaedim, Hunter

Hunter charged at the Dominion. His burning blade could not make contact and he couldn't keep up with the Dominion's moves, he was too fast. The Dominion was playing with him. “So predictable,” he muttered and kicked Hunter in the ribs. Hunter flew back, crashing into several trees. Hunter was down, that kick had broken several of his ribs.

“I know the power that you have, though you don’t wield it nearly as well as your ancestor did.”

“What are you talking about?” said Hunter, who barely had enough strength to look up.

“It was a hundred years ago. There was a man. He was the strongest human I had ever seen, he destroyed many of our cities and killed tens of thousands of Thaedians without remorse. He is the only one that could wound me. He used a special technique. He called it the flaming hydra.”

Hunter was speechless

“This scar you see on my chest was made by that man. I wonder how he’d feel about his legacy being left to you, who can’t even control the power that you have.”

A roar came from the tree. The dragon had woken up, it was trying to escape, and called for assistance. Several other dragons were flying in. The other elves called out to the Dominion He turned, facing the dragon with his ears twitching. He seemed to make a decision, he looked down at Hunter and said, "I will punish you for your family's sins later."

In seconds, he was gone.

As soon as he left, Rowan and Vraya came to get Hunter. Rowan picked Hunter up. Hunter groaned in pain as he was hoisted onto Rowan's back. They saw this as their chance to escape. After they had travelled a sufficient distance away from the battle, they took a break to rest, Rowan put Hunter on the ground gingerly. Vraya checked him over, it seemed that it was only his ribs that had been damaged, but the damage was pretty severe. She bandaged him as best she could. It would take weeks before he could walk properly again.

57

Redall, Brtann

Brtann hesitated in the hallway so long that Lnore finally emerged and nearly walked into him.

She jumped when she saw him. "It can't be," she whispered.

"It is love." Brtann did not move but opened his arms. Within moments Lnore was holding him, nuzzling him affectionately. Restoring their bond. After a few moments of both luxuriating in the chance to touch, let alone see and speak to one another, Lnore pulled back.

Brtann tilted his head quizzically.

"The walls have eyes and ears." Lnore's ears flicked in the direction of a camera near the ceiling.

Brtann backed off. "We need to speak. I'm here to support," it pained him to say it, "our deal with Sunnico."

Lnore's tail thumped on the floor with irritation to hear him say this.

Brtann repeated, "We need to talk. We can speak at home?" He asked hopefully.

Lnore dismissed this with a snort. "I have not lived in the Raven District for two years. It's not safe there. I live in a Sunnico dorm. I guess you will too now."

He cringed to hear her deadened tone. What was keeping her going?

Later, she told him of how, after he disappeared, the safety of the Raven District went from bad to worse, especially for breesians. She'd taken up the offer from Sunnico to move onsite, after life in their old neighbourhood had become unsafe. Greg had insisted on staying in the Raven District, he had taken up residence in their home. Without any of their new Djanian imports coming in, however, the store quickly lost its appeal. He'd been forced to begin stocking it with what was available, and what was available was mostly Sunnico products.

Their shop had become just another casino. Greg had fought it for a long time, but six months ago he finally let Sunnico start pumping their drugs via the ventilation system. It was the only way to keep the gamblers placid. The last time Lnore had seen Greg, he'd reeked of the drugs, and she could spot the signs of addiction.

For Lnore herself, she had continued with the gauntlet implementation plans. She hadn't given any hint of insubordination. She had seen how quickly Danica had been able to cover up the death that had sent Brtann to Djania.

Lnore felt a fool for having sent him away.

She'd worked away the days in the lab that Sunnico had given her, constantly troubleshooting the gauntlets, identifying any number of non-essential flaws to remove or inconsequential add-ons, in hopes of delaying the production as long as possible. As a side project, she'd gotten her hands on some gambling machines and had been altering them, adding vents and air purifiers that would allow the ventilated drugs to be blasted away from the player. She didn't know how much this could help the already addicted, but she believed these modifications might stop the spread of new addictions. She'd managed to sneak plans to Rngal years back and Rngal had been implementing the changes and including a few of the altered models in each shipment, Lnore had made sure that a few had ended up in her old store.

With Brtann back, the couple was upgraded to a suitably larger dorm, but both knew that there was no way to speak unguarded.

On Lnore's eventual day off, they left the Sunnico compound for the first time. They knew that there were Sunnico staff following them, but they had options. They went to the breesian quarter of Redall. They spoke together in their hybrid breesian that merged Djanian and Rominore dialects.

"I was found" Brtann said, "the human, Gina, Rngal and most of all you were at risk. I couldn't say no to Danica."

"Danica can't hurt me. She needs the gauntlets now more than ever. Their attempts to expand the reach of the gambling machines have failed spectacularly. Other cities have seen what is going on in the Raven District and have blocked the sales of the machines. They are being investigated for the link to the drug problems too. Danica needs a legitimate product on the market, and our gauntlets are all she has. I'm sad to hear that they've got Rngal. Last year, I managed to smuggle evidence connecting Sunnico with the decline of the Raven District to Rngal, she has everything. It is too bad she didn't have any way to use it."

Another week passed. Brtann urged Lnore to complete the gauntlets and prepare a package for the Djanian tech hub.

Danica had lost patience with dealing with Lnore years ago, so the two rarely crossed paths anymore. Brtann also hadn't been in any rush to see Danica again and since he'd arrived back in Redall, he'd been meticulously avoiding her. Now, as the gauntlets were completed, he knew that it was finally time to seek Danica out.

58

Prancinia, Gina

As Montel schemed over ways to get Gina back, Gina and Rngal were spending their days at the tech hub. Day in and day out, Gina wasn't given anything to do, so she spent her days exploring the areas of the tech hub that were accessible to her. She found a small library and began looking through some of the non-confidential past research for products that the researchers had done. She saw the long list of failed projects that Sunnico had invested in but had never come to market.

Rngal had been put to work directly. She'd taken up the further implementation of the gauntlet programme. Her insights as the former number two of this operation gave Rngal invaluable knowledge. She had already managed to pause production on many lines to prepare for the gauntlet manufacturing based on the rudimentary specs that they had received so far.

As the days passed Gina and Rngal could only see each other at mealtimes. Through their mental bond, Rngal could tell that Gina was trying to keep busy, but that there was nothing useful for her to do, and Gina could tell that Rngal was overwhelmed with work.

She had offered to help Rngal of course, but backed off when she felt the alarm bells that this suggestion set off in Rngal's mind. Sunnico was involved in something bad, something that Rngal felt was better to keep from Gina. After a little while, Rngal shared some of the incomplete blueprints of the gauntlets. Gina studied them, she was not an engineer, but she was learning quickly. Discussing the gauntlets with Rngal was fascinating.

Just two weeks after they'd arrived, Rngal had hit a wall in her attempt to prepare the factories for gauntlet production. Rngal was doing everything she could to stop production all together in the factories. By single-mindedly pursuing the implementation of the gauntlets, she was re-directing the resources away from the gambling machines. And because the plans were incomplete, there was no way that the gauntlets could go into production. Factory output was slowing, which was exactly what Rngal wanted. Gina could tell that Rngal was trying to move very slowly to buy time. She sensed as well, that Rngal was waiting for news from Brtann.

A commotion outside the tech hub caught Gina's attention, a sleek vehicle appeared just outside the compound. It cruised through the security gate, parking in front of the entrance. It was a Djanian vehicle that had been adapted for human use.

Montel emerged from the vehicle. Gina watched him walk into the Sunnico headquarters unchallenged. Only moments later, Gina was summoned to a conference room.

A human Sunnico executive stood with Montel and Rngal.

"Rngal, Gina," Montel said, nodding to both of them, "I'm here to tell you that Sunnico and Denma have reached an agreement. Gina is an employee of Denma, she will need to return to us."

Gina didn't know how to react. It was clear she had no role at Sunnico and would only have the slightest access to Rngal's work. Gina wasn't certain that she even wanted to know more, after having understood fragments from her connection with Rngal.

When she'd invoked the phana, she'd naively thought they'd go back to Ypare and continue their work there. Not that they would both be trapped in a Sunnico compound, with minimal opportunity to interact. Gina was bored and confused. For the first time since arriving in Djania, she wanted to go home. Was that what Montel was offering?

"The phana can accommodate short periods of separation, if both parties are willing." Montel contributed. Gina nodded, she remembered this from his book.

"Is someone willing?" Montel asked in surprisingly fluent Djanian to Rngal.

Rngal tried to focus her senses on Gina. Their telepathic connection had grown stronger in the weeks since the invocation of the phana. Gina seemed hopeful, but was it hopeful to stay with Rngal? Or was it hopeful to be gone from this place?

She took a guess: "This one has work, but fears that her phana companion is not content. This one will not presume to decide for the other."

Gina looked at Rngal, Rngal looked back at her, flicking her ears forward in an encouraging gesture.

Gina took the opportunity: "This one will accept a short separation. But only if this one may see our remaining companion."

Montel stared hard at Gina. She had backed him into a corner. "This one grants the request," he said.

Rngal said: "The phana cannot be broken. It will be revived soon."

Gina echoed the traditional phrase. The room again shimmered around them briefly, and Gina felt her mind entirely her own for the first time in weeks. It was a deeply lonely feeling.

With that, Montel swept Gina out of the room and into his vehicle. They travelled in silence back to Denma HQ. Gina did not have many possessions to speak of, but Montel had still taken care to have everything moved, from her home in Ypare to a small flat near the Denma building. He brought Gina there.

Montel knew that Sunnico had taken Brtann to Redall, on Nüland. Now, he had to figure out how to get Gina there as well. He'd met Danica a handful of times, perhaps he could persuade her somehow.

He made the plans to travel with Gina to Redall.

59

Thaedim, Hunter

Hunter, Rowan and Vraya travelled further into elven territory, avoiding the cities. Vraya had adapted a few of her remaining drones to carry Hunter as his ribs healed. They had almost arrived at the garden.

The Eternal Garden contained all sorts of plants and herbs. According to Frithe clan legends, the garden had herbs that could grant you immortality and others that could make you stronger. Rowan was hoping that these legends might be true. Hunter was focused on finding some benthe to stop his ribs from aching. They had been on the move for a week.

Eventually, they arrived before a large, ornate gate, scattered around the gate were skeletons of fallen warriors from the Thaedim War. Clearly, members of every species had fallen here, from dragons to breesians. The garden was just beyond. All they had to do was open the gate.

Rowan was ready to push it open, but Vraya stopped him, "Wait, maybe there's a trap." she said.

Rowan carefully looked around but didn't find any sign of a trap, Vraya scanned the area with her drones but also didn't pick up on anything. Rowan pushed the gate and it slowly swung open. They headed inside but froze just after entering. Behind the gate there was nothing, only the ashes of plants and a burned tree in the middle. “What could have done this?” said Vraya. The air was filled with a strong smell.

Hunter recognized the scent; it was the same earthy odour as the drugs from Redall. Whoever or whatever had been creating monsters in Redall, had also callously destroyed the Eternal Garden. With it, they also made Hunter's and Rowan's quest impossible to complete. None of the clans would be able to continue their tradition. He wanted to make the ones responsible answer for this destruction.

“I know this smell,” said Hunter, “It was all over the creature that I killed in Redall. It was probably someone from Nüland who was behind the destruction of the Eternal Garden.”

He looked around at the destruction and said, “No wonder the elves hate us.”

Vraya and Rowan stayed silent.

Hunter turned to his companions and said: “I’m going back to Redall, to find out who did this. What will you two do from here?”

“Redall huh? It’s been a while since I was last there, but I have a score to settle with the creature that killed my brother. I’m in!” Rowan said

“I’m also coming, since that seems to be the only chance, I have left to get that power source plant.” said Vraya

Hunter looked at his companions, “I guess that settles it. The next stop is Redall!”

60

Redall, Brtann

"Danica, a word?"

"Brtann, I'm in the middle of something."

"It'll only take a moment and I think you'll be very pleased to hear what I have to say."

That made her look up. "Okay, let's talk."

Brtann entered Danica's office. "I've worked with Lnore, and she's finalised the plans for the gauntlets, even upgraded them in ways that will make them even more useful as products for breesians. She also has a new prototype that will help the team in Prancinia."

"Brtann, that *is* excellent news. Where are these plans? The new prototypes?"

"Ready to be shipped. Lnore prepared everything in Djanian, your technicians there should have no problems understanding them."

Danica looked mildly annoyed but brushed it off. "When will it go?"

"Later today - the airship service has already been planned. It will get there as soon as possible. I had a copy prepared for you. Here." He handed her the blueprints and a single prototype gauntlet.

“Very efficient.” She nodded him away as she opened the blueprints that she had no hopes of understanding.

When Brtann left her office, Danica gave instructions to follow the package, but she hadn’t foreseen Brtann’s connections. He had made sure that the package was already well on its way before he’d gone in to speak to her.

Another week passed uneventfully for Brtann and Lnore. Now that their blueprints were flying to Djania, they had a moment of calm. Sunnico's focus was off them for a moment.

It was time for Brtann to return to the Raven District with Lnore. When he saw the derelict storefronts and the trash on the street, he couldn't believe that this was the same neighbourhood. Only a decade ago, they had moved in, full of hope. They approached the old shop. Brtann opened the door but immediately recoiled: he could smell the leftover, earthy stink of the drugs. Lnore came up beside him.

“You’ll be ok. There aren’t any drugs before the evening. It’s a new rule in Redall.”

“What...?”

“The authorities couldn’t control the addiction, but they could control when the addicts get their fix. They’ve made it a rule for all casinos that air vents cannot be used until the evening. If the air vents can’t be used, the drugs can’t get airborne. A few dealers have sprung up with copycat inhalers, but the effect is not the same.” Lnore said it without emotion. It was an accepted fact.

They stepped into the hazy remnants of their old store. Greg was waiting for them.

He was a shadow of his former self. He’d always been thin and a little scruffy, but he looked shrunken and hollowed out, with dark circles under his eyes.

"Brtann!" He pushed out from the back of the store feebly. "I heard you were back. I'm so glad to see you!" Greg hugged him awkwardly. Brtann patted Greg's back gently. He seemed so fragile.

"Greg, how are you doing? Lnore told me what happened here."

"I'm getting by. And you know, I think things are looking up. I knew this couldn't go on forever. Now that we're back together, we'll make it right! Get back to managing the store together. Right?" Greg's eyes seemed to glisten with unshed tears as he wished for his old life, a life free from addiction.

"I hope so, Greg." Brtann said. "Can I see the rest of the place? The workshop? The flat?"

"Of course!" Greg returned to a version of his former self and led them on a tour of their old home. The store was the only thing he'd changed, and even that only after Lnore's agreement. Which she'd given immediately when she saw that it was the only way Greg could make a living. Lnore had also not stopped Greg from signing with Sunnico for the pharma 'trials', as they called them. She'd heard about the contracts, and she'd seen the damage it was doing to him. Just a short distance away, at the Sunnico compound, she'd lived in relative security. While Greg had been left in the middle of it. She'd invited him to join her many times, but, stubbornly, he'd taken it on himself to protect their old life.

When they entered the flat, they saw how meagre Greg's life had become. There was minimal food and only small comforts to make it a home for himself. In the early days, when there'd still been some hope that the store would bounce back, he'd started selling off his prized gauntlet collection in the store. Only one pair remained now. Old battle gauntlets, antiques almost, they were in nearly pristine condition. One had a vicious spear embedded, the other had a shield that could be ejected towards the opponent.

They stayed to have tea, the three of them reunited. Brtann explained to Greg what had happened to him.

As they emerged from the shop, evening was beginning to fall. Greg's haunted face began to have a look of craving. He knew his next hit was soon. He just needed to wait a little longer.

Despite the sweat of anticipation, they saw starting to form on Greg's forehead, he insisted on walking them to the edge of the Raven District.

Just as they were about to step back into Redall's main district, it happened. Both Brtann and Lnore heard the attacker just before he could strike. Lnore shoved Brtann out of the way, just as a powerful punch landed, demolishing the wall that they had been walking in front of.

61

Redall, Hunter

“How are we going to get to Redall?” Rowan asked.

“We could go back the same way we came.” Hunter suggested.

Vraya laughed, “Going back the way we came? Look around, I still have parts of my broken drones and there are other materials here that I can use. I could repair them and attach handlebars underneath so they can fly us back to the coast. There are only two problems for this brilliant solution of mine: you two. You will need to be back to full strength to be able to hold on.” She said looking at Hunter, “And you,” she continued looking at Rowan, “will need to get over your fear of heights.” Rowan groaned.

“I’ll recover so quick, you’ll think I’m from the Strannae clan. Faster than you can modify those brilliant drones of yours.” Hunter challenged playfully, but regretted it as a sharp pang in his ribs nearly had him doubled over.

“I can be your assistant for the rebuilding, just let me know what I can do.” Rowan offered.

“If I'm right, you should recover in about a month Hunter. And just a warning, it won’t be comfortable dangling off the drones. But it’ll get us back to the coast faster than any other method, and we’ll meet fewer enemies along the way.”

“Sounds to me like we have a plan.” Hunter said

The weeks passed, Hunter's ribs healed, and Vraya finished the modifications to her drones. When they were ready, the trio departed, dangling off the drones in short bursts, more hopping than flying. Rowan hated every minute of their trip back to the coast, but he couldn't help but be impressed by the amount of work Vraya had done in such a short time. Hunter managed to lead them back to his small motorboat. It was cramped for three passengers and Vraya’s backpack full of drones and tools. But it managed to stay afloat.

After they arrived on the coast of Nüland, they made their way to Redall. Once there, they spent a few days combing the city, spending time in the Raven District, looking around the casinos. They saw the drugs being pumped through the air vents at the gamblers and the way people would stumble home. But they didn't come across any of the mutated, feral creatures Hunter had encountered during his first time in the city.

Rowan was on high alert, looking for his brother’s killer.

Near dusk one evening, something caught Rowan’s eye. “The grey bastard!” he spat and charged full speed at two breesians, cracking his knuckles.

PART 8 - JUSTICE

62

Redall, Brtann

"Murderer!" shouted Rowan, as he pivoted from his first attack on Brtann.

He lunged again, going straight for Brtann. For the first time, Brtann feared that he would need to use all of the power Lnore had engineered into his gauntlets. This assailant was clearly powerful.

Brtann managed to dodge again. Rowan smashed into a wall again, but he was back up on his feet immediately

Brtann couldn't keep this up for long. A third time, Rowan came at him with those deadly fists. Brtann managed to catch one fist with his gauntlet. But the second fist went slamming into his side. Brtann was knocked off his feet, but didn't let go of the fist. He managed to twist Rowan, flipping him with the movement and knocking them both off balance. Before Rowan could come back at him again, he swiped with his free hand, claws out. He managed to land a strike but held back from using full force. He didn't want to be responsible for murder ever again.

Rowan groaned when the claws struck his flesh, but that didn't stop him from attacking. "The grey beast!" He spat. "You're the one they talked about when Dan was found mauled! I know that you did it, I know they covered it up! And now you dare come back here? Well, you won't be around for long." His next punch landed hard on Brtann's face, snapping his neck backwards.

"Lnore! Catch!" Greg called out. He had run back to the house and grabbed the battle gauntlets, now tossing them to Lnore.

Out of nowhere a flash of silver swiped by Rowan's face. Lnore's spear had just missed.

"Oh no you don't." Vraya said, dropping a drone to intercept the spear. Lnore swung the shield viciously, slicing the drone in half and twisting the movement at the last second to launch it towards Vraya.

Vraya jumped out of the way easily. "Hah! there's fun to be had on Nüland, after all."

Vraya made quick work of neutralising the battle gauntlets, but she didn't push the advantage. This one wasn't a threat to Rowan, and it would have been too easy. Vraya tried to avoid fighting other breesians, she didn't enjoy hurting her own kind. As she pinned the other breesian, her eyes glimpsed a woven Rominore necklace. We're the same, she thought, and she loosened her grip, but did not let go.

Rowan continued to pummel Brtann, as Lnore found herself weaponless in front of Vraya.

Hunter watched the fight unfold.

63

Redall, Hunter

"Brtann!"

Hunter started at the familiar voice, he turned and was shocked to see Gina. Peripherally, he also clocked a half-elven man behind her. It seemed he was hard wired to notice Thaedians now.

"Gina!" He called, "don't get involved, this isn't your fight!"

"Hunter! What...? No! You have to stop them!"

"Not on your life! We'd level half the neighbourhood if I fought Rowan."

"At least stop him from killing Brtann! Whatever it is, it's not *his* fault! It's Sunnico! They are drugging the people of the Raven District."

Hunter turned back to where Rowan was pummeling Brtann, who seemed nearly unconscious. He'd trusted Rowan's version of events, but he also trusted his childhood friend. And after their investigations of the last few days, Gina's story made sense. After the slightest deliberation, he made his move.

It only took a heartbeat for him to have his sword out and be standing between his companions and the two breesians they'd easily overpowered.

"Ok Rowan, Vraya. You've had your fun. Now it's time to stop."

Vraya shrugged, not willing to challenge Hunter, and stepped back, freeing Lnore.

Rowan shook his head "Not this time, Hunter, this monster killed Dan." And he charged straight towards Hunter.

Hunter knew he didn't want to hurt Rowan but was not used to the art of gentle disarmament of his opponents. Especially when his opponent's weapon was his fists.

Hunter used the blade to keep Rowan at a distance, just offering mild cuts to keep him at bay. "Gina, take your friends and run."

Gina moved to where Brtann lay in a heap and tried to pull him away.

"Hunter, you don't know what you're doing; he's getting away!" Rowan yelled and tried to get at Brtann again. Hunter blocked him with a deep cut to his cheek.

"Rowan, stand down, don't make this worse than it needs to be."

"YOU. DON'T. UNDERSTAND!" Rowan yelled, and he punched the ground between him and Hunter. The road cracked open with a tremor that threw Hunter off balance. Chunks of rock and boulders floated up from the broken surface, surrounding Rowan. He concentrated on Hunter and all the rocks went flying at lightning speed towards Hunter. Every rock that was sent Hunter's way was replaced by another one, pulled up from the ground.

Hunter made his decision without thinking. He sliced through as many of the rocks and boulders as he could. He could feel his sword dulling under the constant bombardment. A few smaller rocks got past his sword, ripping through his skin. He absorbed as much as he could, so that they wouldn't damage the city around them.

The force and the volume of rocks that Rowan was furiously shooting his way nearly knocked him off his feet, he was reminded of the Dominion's pressure.

"Rowan... you... you've Awakened." He said and flew forward, sword ready to strike.

64

Redall, Vraya

Vraya watched cautiously from a short distance away. She saw the new human run to the injured breesians and try to help them up. Another, sickly looking human appeared from an alleyway, he was the one Vraya had seen bring the battle gauntlets to the fight. Now, he tried to pull the Rominore breesian to safety, but he was too weak.

The elf stepped forward. Instinctively, Vraya activated her drones targets set on the elf, they might be her only way out of this fight.

To her astonishment, he didn't even look at her. The elf went straight to the injured breesians and lifted both with a strength that Vraya had seen before. Anyone who had been to Thaedim would not have been surprised, it was common knowledge there that that elves were capable of immense strength. Vraya, who stood on the side-lines of the battle between Hunter and Rowan, deactivated her drones as the elf turned away, counting herself lucky that he hadn't joined the fight. That might have made the odds a little different.

Vraya watched the group until the elf was out of sight. She turned back to the battle raging between her companions.

Rowan started to show signs of tiring, and the storm of rocks was slowing. He must have exhausted himself with this level of clan magic. Hunter lunged forward, sword raised, but rather than slicing his friend he turned his wrist at the last moment and knocked Rowan on the head with the hilt of his sword, sending him into oblivion.

Hunter turned to Vraya. "Can you look after him? I need to see about my friend."

"Sure," said Vraya. "But watch out. They have an elf on their side."

"Half-elf. But yeah, I caught that too. See you later."

65

Redall, Lnore

Lnore was conscious as she was carried away from the place where they had been attacked. But she could see that Brtann had passed out.

The man that carried them started to speak to the human trailing behind him. She must be Gina, Lnore thought.

"There's a Denma-owned hospital not far from here that will be safer than any of the public hospitals." He did not mention going to a Sunnico medical centre, for obvious reasons.

Gina ran to catch what he was saying. "Thank you." she said simply and followed him. Greg was a few steps behind the group.

When they arrived at the hospital, Montel gently lowered Lnore into a chair, but held on to Brtann, who, unconscious, might've incurred further damage by being placed in a chair.

Lnore's managed to see his pointed ears as he moved away. She wondered what else he was capable of; he didn't seem tired at all.

He went to the reception and made a phone call, within minutes of putting the phone down doctors and nurses came streaming toward them. Brtann was suddenly their top priority.

Brtann was taken into surgery urgently.

Lnore had only minor injuries that were cleaned up easily. Back in the waiting room she met Gina, having heard stories about her from Brtann. She noted the Rominore necklace wrapped around Gina's wrist and remembered some of the stories Brtann had told her about life in Ypare. How did she just convince the opponent's leader to step in and stop his friend from killing Brtann? Gina could be a new and important ally.

At that moment, the doctors and nurses saw Greg. The signs of addiction were clear. They couldn't force him to stay at the hospital, but a nurse still gently suggested it. Greg pushed back, insisting he was fine. But Lnore stepped forward. "Greg, I think it would be for the best if you stayed here."

"But the store..." He protested weakly.

"We're going to fix that. You've done enough, now you need to rest."

Somehow Lnore saying it out loud, allowed him to collapse. He was quickly laid out in a hospital bed, and the doctor began a check-up to see how far gone he was.

66

Redall, Hunter

Hunter appeared at the entrance of the hospital. He'd followed Gina and the others through the city.

"Gina!" Hunter called.

She turned, "Hunter, what are you doing here? You're hanging out with criminals now!?"

"It's a long story, and they're not criminals. They're good people, we've been through a lot together. They've got my back."

"Like I don't?" Gina asked.

"Yeah, yeah, you'd think your way out of a problem, but in a fight, you'd just drag us down."

"Well, my thinking got us out of a lot of trouble as kids." She retorted.

"There are some things we've seen on Thaedim that you couldn't wrap your head around, let alone think through. There's no thinking there, it's just fighting."

"On Thaedim? Don't tell me you went there after all! Did you find out about yourself? What you are?"

"Sort of. But wait," Hunter concentrated on Gina for a second, "Magic? Are you caught in some spell?"

"What? How did you ...?"

"Clan kid." Hunter grinned.

"Right." Gina should have knows someone raised in the warrior system would be able to tell. She continued, "And well sort of ... um ... yes. it's called the phana, there's magic on Breeland. I-I managed to invoke a spell." Gina said, both proud and sheepish.

"We're going to talk about that. But first you need to explain. I knocked Rowan out, but when he wakes up, he's gonna need a better explanation than 'Sunnico's responsible'. What happened? How did his brother end up dead? And how are you hanging out with elves now?"

"I'll start with the easy one. The elf, Montel, he's half-elf, well I think so anyway, he works at Denma, he's my boss actually."

"An elf working at a human corporation? I don't believe that for a second, he could level a city with a thought. He doesn't need to bother with human society."

"*Half*-elf, Montel doesn't talk about any of that with me. But *you're* welcome to bring it up with him sometime." Gina sighed. Now, she needed to get to the difficult part. She didn't know the whole story; she'd only gotten snippets from her connection with Rngal. "I don't know the details. Brtann, the guy your friend nearly put into a coma, knows what happened."

"The murderer?"

"Don't be like that."

Lnore's sensitive ears had been tracking the conversation. Montel had too. He'd been pleased to hear Gina defending him. Maybe he'd gained some trust with her after all. Was this the moment to divulge what his spies had discovered? They weren't his secrets to tell.

Lnore had no such concerns. She crossed the room quickly and stood near Hunter and Gina.

"I think I can help you." Lnore shared the story of the drugs and the gambling machines. How the night that Rowan's brother died, both had been heavily drugged, from Sunnico's illegal drug testing programme. Brtann had never seen Rowan's brother before and Dan was so addicted that he was near-dead anyway. He was skeletal, having stopped eating almost entirely, with barely enough energy to stay upright behind a gambling console. He had been on his way to a casino for his next fix when he slammed into Brtann.

Sunnico had covered up the tragedy of what had happened almost immediately, but their only goal had been to save their drug trial. They had no particular interest in covering up Brtann's responsibility, which is how the rumours of Dan having been killed by a grey breesian managed to get out to Rowan, despite the lockdown on information.

"It devastated Brtann to know what had happened. But it wasn't his fault. It was the fault of the drugs. And also, the fault of the gauntlets. Gauntlets that I created. Without those, there's no way he would have been strong enough to fight off a man in his drug-hazed state." Lnore looked down to where she held Brtann's gauntlets. Her own hands were bare after having her gauntlets disabled during the fight with Vraya. She'd removed Brtann's gauntlets before surgery. Lnore could have put them on, they would have adjusted to her slightly smaller hand size, but it didn't feel right.

"The last time I was here, it was pretty bleak. I was also attacked by...someone who must have been on those drugs." Hunter said. "But you said Sunnico, right? I heard about them when I was here before, now that I think about it, I've seen their logo before. Maybe. Um... I think my mom might have something to do with it…" Hunter trailed off. He remembered the packet of papers that had tumbled out of the envelope. He reached into his backpack and pulled out the envelope. The same papers came out, but he noticed now that there had also been a letter in with the other papers. He started reading.

67

Redall, Hunter

Dear Hunter,

With this letter, I've included some of my findings from having worked in Redall for Sunnico.

I survived a year on Thaedim. I fought my way through to the Eternal Garden and I found the benthe plant. I brought a few samples of it back with me.

And then I went to Redall. After fighting every day for a year, I was tired. I wanted the warrior age to end. I wanted to give the peacetime era a chance. It seemed to be another path to success.

But I was wrong.

Sunnico forced me to do terrible experiments that would have maimed me if I could have been burned. I hid my Talent so that they wouldn't push me further. My colleagues were not so lucky. They didn't tell us what we were working on or how it contributed to their products. I had been there for about two years when I'd singed my hands particularly badly in an experiment earlier in the day.

While I was waiting for the effects of the burn to wear off, I overheard some other technicians talking nearby, they mentioned the upcoming human trials of a new drug. Usually, this was the final phase of a drug's development, and it meant that the drug was stable. They spoke about how this one might be a success. They said that the only side effects that they'd found were some rare, violent outbursts. But the euphoric sensations were confirmed.

So many times, I wished I'd never found out the truth of what was happening, and never interfered at all.

I continued to eavesdrop on their conversations. That was when I heard that there were worrying signs of addiction, but they'd been told to continue the trials.

I never thought that skills that I'd learned to fight demons would help me to get to the side of the compound where the trials were taking place. I saw the blank eyes and deadened faces of the trial participants. I tried to speak to one of them. I went back, day after day, sometimes trying to offer them food or some company. But they did not acknowledge me. The only time they seemed to react was when the next dose was due. I gave up and returned to my lab. I tried to continue my job, but the trials would not leave my mind. Since I had been in Redall, I had grown a small garden and found that the benthe plant grew well in the soil there. I had begun to study its properties, including pain relief. I wondered if it could help the experiment subjects.

So, I snuck into their area again and offered them benthe tea. Somehow, benthe, when added to the chemicals in the drug, gave hallucinations, and they could fight through pain and injuries.

It didn't take long for the technicians to extract this new compound from the test subjects' samples and incorporate it into the drug's ingredients. When the benthe molecules combined with the other chemicals, it had a horrific effect, it caused bizarre mutations in some of the test subjects, turning their hands into long claw-like fingers, which always came with the losing of their minds and personalities. Many of the test subjects were isolated to keep from killing each other.

I had contributed to Sunnico's super drug. I burned my benthe garden to the ground.

I had to leave. This new way of life was worse than the warrior times.

I tried so many times to tell the authorities, but no one listened.

So, I went home, started a family and raised you in the clan tradition. At least as warriors, we were fighting demons. Sunnico was finding ways to enslave our own kind. From then on,

I was convinced that the old ways were better.

Here, I've given you Sunnico's company secrets. I hope that you can do what I failed to do: make Sunnico pay for the pain they've inflicted.

You know I'm always on your side.

Love

Mom

Hunter looked at the letter and then looked at the pages underneath that his mom had included. He couldn't make sense of it. He did what he'd always done when he'd felt out of his depths, he gave it to Gina.

But Gina was not a scientist, she couldn't make sense of the formulas. She kept sifting through the pages until she found the notes on the human experiments. She shuddered as she read them.

"This is awful" She breathed. "We need to tell someone. Shut it down."

Hunter knew there was a way to end it. But warrior clans were strictly forbidden to hurt humans.

Hunter re-read his mother's letter. It seemed that she was urging just one course of action. He thought about Rowan's grief and anger about his brother and Brtann's deep anguish about what he'd done. To Hunter, the course was clear. Sunnico could not stand.

68

Redall, Hunter

Hunter stood.

“Where is Sunnico?” He asked quietly, with the authority that the Awakened power brings.

Lnore stood. “I’ll show you,” she said.

They arrived in what felt like moments. Hunter stood outside the gates to the pharma empire. Lnore stood beside him.

“I can get you in.” She said softly.

“No” he replied, “It’s not necessary, but it would be good of you to get back to the hospital, I think that will be outside the range of what’s about to happen.”

“What’s about to happen...” Lnore echoed and then nodded, this was right, “Yes, give me 15 minutes and then go.”

Hunter waited patiently, although his mind was on fire. The wars with demons had ended, only for humans to do experiments and enslave each other for lack of an enemy.

His rage grew as he stood still. Blue flames surrounded him.

Hunter gave up on trying to control himself. He hoped that Lnore had gotten far enough away, and that Gina was safe.

He let go.

He let the full force of his power hit the entry gates into the Sunnico campus. They blasted into nothing. Hunter walked in. He directed his flames towards the buildings on either side and before long, he realised that the flames had surrounded him, like a multi-headed hydra. A power that he'd never imagined allowed him to burn everything in sight. He'd managed to engulf the entire campus in flames in just minutes. He stood in the centre of the grounds, directing the flaming heads of the hydra to each building until they were all lit up.

One by one, the buildings exploded, and the chemical compounds reacted to his blue flames. There was no control, no finesse. He saw a tower at the far end of the compound beginning to collapse in on itself. He laughed. He couldn't be sure, but he hoped that the ones responsible were in the buildings. As everything burned, Hunter revelled in his power. If there were buildings that weren't burning fast enough, he called the flames higher. Until there were only charred bricks remaining.

He would destroy it all.

But then he heard it. Human screams. He saw the people burned alive with his flames. Some were researchers responsible for the pain and suffering. Hunter felt no remorse.

But then he came upon the barracks of human test subjects, crippled and insane from Sunnico's experiments. He saw the innocents screaming and, although he knew, in some way, he was offering a kindness in death, their screams reached into his soul.

His flames evaporated.

But it left only charred remains. Hunter had destroyed the entire compound within moments.

He snapped back to attention. He had to get away, no one could know what he had done.

He tried to run, but after exerting this kind of power, he could only move slowly.

Montel, however, had arranged for a quick getaway.

He arrived within moments of the flames dying, “Hunter,” he yelled from the driver’s seat, “get in!”

Hunter, still dazed from fully using his powers, stumbled towards the vehicle.

Montel drove the vehicle to an airship that Denma had offered him for his personal use.

He pushed Hunter onto the airship and said, “We'll meet you in Djania. Don't worry, you're safe.” The doors to the airship closed, and Hunter passed out.

PART 9 - RESET

69

Redall, Vraya

After Hunter ran off, Vraya looked down at the unconscious Rowan. "Well, I guess it's up to me then." She muttered as she picked him up and started walking out of the Raven District. She covered ground quickly, about an hour into her journey she sensed a change in the air. Her ears twitched and she noticed how the bustle of the city seemed to slow around her. A second later, an explosion from the other side of the city rippled through the air and nearly blasted her off her feet.

"Hunter!" She could smell the same burning smell from when Hunter fought the Dominion. She changed direction, with the still unconscious Rowan.

She reached the outskirts of the now destroyed Sunnico HQ just as the flames died down. She could smell the same earthy odour from the Eternal Garden, these were clearly the ones that had destroyed it.

From a distance, she saw Hunter staggering towards a vehicle. Through the window of the vehicle, she saw the elf who had carried the injured breesians away. Hunter fell into the vehicle, which disappeared at speed the second the door had closed behind him. She considered giving chase, but feeling Rowan's heavy weight on her shoulders, she knew that even with breesian speed and agility she could not keep up. And there was no way she was willing to challenge an elf.

"You're on your own now Hunter. I hope you won't regret it," she said to herself as she turned her back on Redall.

By morning, Vraya had reached the coast and retrieved the motorboat they had hidden in a quiet cave on the beach. Rowan started groaning as she pushed the boat out in the water.

"Vraya, a boat? What?"

"Go back to sleep Rowan, I'll wake you when we're home."

70

Prancinia, Gina

When Hunter woke up, his eyes landed on a familiar face.

"Mom? What? Where are we? I'm… home?"

"Hunter, you're awake!" Robyn said, "a lot has happened; you've been in and out of consciousness for a week now. We'll have time to explain."

Hunter fell back asleep.

The next time he woke up, he saw Gina. "Gina? Did we really go home?"

"Hell no Hunter. We're in Djania. Montel has found us a place to hide while the Nüland authorities try to sort out what happened to the Sunnico compound. Rumours of the warrior clans being Awakened are starting to take hold. Governments across our continent and -who knows- maybe beyond, would love to control that power. It's important that none of them get their hands on you."

"Hah! As if they could get me to do something I don't want to do," Hunter scoffed, returning to his usual, over-confident self.

"Maybe so, but still, better not to test that theory." she replied, "if it hadn't been for Montel's quick thinking, you might've been caught already."

"The elf," Hunter grumbled.

"*Half*-elf" Gina corrected, but she knew he was doing it on purpose, she could tell that this would become another one of their running jokes.

"But my mom, why is she here?"

"I went to get her. After the complete meltdown of Sunnico HQ, I thought only Robyn would be able to explain what being Awakened means and how to deal with the after effects. Well maybe your grandpa too, but he was too frail to make the trip."

Hunter nodded, Gina's logic was solid, as always. "Yeah, I'll need to talk to her."

"Definitely, but first: eat! I've got curry or toffee squares, you choose."

"Curry. Toffee is nasty."

Gina felt relieved that he was revived enough to remember his distaste for her favourite snack. She handed him a trayl and he ate with ravenous speed, cleaning the bowl in minutes.

"That was good. Thanks"

"It's good to see you eat. Your mom told us that the first time a Veronn clan member fully accesses their magic it knocks them out. She said that you'll need to learn how to control it better."

"How can I do that? It's been three generations since the last member of my family was Awakened!"

"Your mom brought some books, books that she's studying right now, to try to help you."

"And what about dad? Did he come too?"

"No, your mom thought it would be safer for him, since he's not from the clan, to stay out of the way. When I told her what happened, she and your grandpa started ordering the rest of your family to go into hiding. That way, they can't be found and interrogated or pressured to give the government information about you. I mean if you think about it, there are a lot of governments that see you as a weapon that they can exploit."

"Can you slow down? This is too much information."

"Sorry! Sorry, you're right I'm going too fast. Better that you rest some more."

"Where's my sword?"

"Just over here, your mom said you'd ask for it."

"Can you bring it over?"

She laid the Sanalia blade next to Hunter on the bed. Somehow being closer to it seemed to relax him. He drifted back to sleep.

Later that day, Gina sat down to a meal with Montel. They'd spent a lot of time together on the trip. The way he'd cared for Brtann and Hunter had given her a new opinion of him. He was thoughtful and considerate, especially with Robyn. He'd set them up in a discreet residence that he kept just on the outskirts of Prancinia. He'd bought it many years ago, on one of his early trips to Djania for Denma. It remained a secret getaway whenever he needed some time to himself. This was the first time that he'd ever brought guests to the house.

"Your dad was an elf, and your mom was a Wanyd clan warrior? And she was the one that started the tradition of training on Thaedim..." Gina was piecing the puzzle together, "And so you have both elven powers and your clan's Talent?"

Montel shrugged, "Maybe. I don't know. I've never trained, I've never wanted to train. My mother turned her back on that life."

“But there’s no way a human could carry two full grown breesians, and you carried Brtann and Lnore to the hospital.”

“Oh. That. Right. Well, I am stronger than my build might suggest, I also have better than average hearing.”

“Stronger than you look? I think it's a lot more than that,” Gina said. Montel looked uncomfortable. “Anything else?”

“I can breathe underwater.”

“Right. The Wanyd clan Talent, of course.”

Montel had had enough of this interrogation, “How do you know so much about the clans? And Thaedim? Most people your age don’t care. Even in your parent’s generation, they stopped caring long ago, someone *your* age shouldn’t know about of any of this.”

“My parent’s generation…How old *are* you?”

“80. Answer the question”

“You don’t look a day over 25.” Gina teased, Montel rolled his eyes, she continued, “I grew up with Hunter, he’s my best friend, and he’s not great at book learning, so whenever he needed to remember something about the warrior clans, he asked me for help. I’ve read all the clan histories and seen all of their secret maps of Thaedim. Studying is kind of my thing.”

“I’ve noticed. Can I ask about your parents? They’re not *only* from Grantan, right?”

Gina sighed, “My mom is from Grantan, my dad is Raninali.” But it didn’t sting as much as that question usually did, maybe because it was coming just after Montel’s own sharing about his parents. And his story was much more complex than her own.

Montel did not dig further, and instead turned the subject to something that he was very curious about: "Did you memorise my entire book on the phana?" he asked.

"Of course not! I just took particularly detailed notes of certain chapters."

"I'm fascinated by your experience as a non-breesian that has managed to invoke it. What is it like?"

"It… it's hard to describe," Gina said honestly, but then changed the subject, "Why were you so fascinated by it?"

"That's enough digging into my past. Let's eat." Montel said, picking up a fork.

71

Redall, Lnore

Montel had given instructions at the Denma hospital for Brtann and Greg to be treated with the utmost care. After his surgery, Brtann woke up, his body aching, He'd had some internal bleeding and a few broken ribs. Other than that, it was mostly bad bruising.

Lnore had been staying with him in the hospital. The Denma staff were under strict orders from Montel to shield the three of them from any investigations or possible harm. If it were to be discovered that she had been the only Sunnico collaborator to survive the explosions, unpleasant questions would come up. She had never been an employee, just a consultant, solely involved in the gauntlet project. As the investigations began, Lnore was content to lay low inside the hospital.

It seemed to be a bit of a farce, watching the news as reports and hear that rumours of arson were flying around, when it was clear as day that it had been magic that had destroyed the Sunnico pharmaceutical hub. But no government wanted to be the first to state this publicly, as they were likely looking for the Veronn clan member that had been Awakened.

Lnore was glad that Montel had acted quickly, with an escape plan that would hopefully mean that this power was not used again.

Lnore and Brtann finally felt free from Sunnico's heavy hand.

On the third day in the hospital, Brtann was well enough to ask about Greg.

Lnore's ears flicked back, and her tail curled slightly. "I tried to visit him, but the staff said I couldn't. He's going through withdrawals, and he is not himself. The doctors said he wouldn't thank us for seeing him like that. They said that he may be here for months, to truly kick the addiction. Because he was exposed so relentlessly as the manager of a casino, his case is especially bad."

"Once we're out of here," Brtann said slowly, thoughtfully, "I want to go back to the Raven District. It's our home. I want to undo what Sunnico did. When he's better, we'll welcome Greg back too. He's family."

72

Prancinia, Montel

Montel's and Gina's role in the re-emergence of the Awakened was not known yet and Montel certainly planned to keep it that way.

He was torn. He'd had a simple objective when this project began. But Hunter had changed the game when he destroyed half of Sunnico. There would be jockeying to fill the gap.

Montel could use this to Denma's benefit, or he could strike out on his own to fill this gap in the market.

Or, an evil part of his mind said, he could manipulate Hunter. This was untold power, that emerges once in a generation, and it had practically fallen into his lap.

The way forward wasn't yet clear to him. He had to fight his elven ancestry that urged him to retire into solitude to contemplate his options. He had to think like a human right now. He didn't entirely trust his own instincts, so he turned to Gina.

"You want my advice?" Gina asked.

"I- well- it's hard to explain. If the clans are Awakening, the world order as we know it is changing. And I've seen your instincts, they're good. I'd like your input on our next move." Montel said.

"S-sure. How can I help?"

"It's been more than a week since Sunnico pharma was destroyed on Nüland. There's still Sunnico tech on Breeland. You've spent time on the inside there. What is your understanding? Does it also need to be destroyed, or can it be salvaged?"

"Destroyed… you can't mean using his powers again! Hunter is not a weapon!" Gina was shocked that Montel might share some of the ideas that she feared others were already thinking.

"Well," Montel said sadly, "there are many now that will see him that way."

Gina's face fell, not because she disagreed, but because she knew it was true. "We need to talk to Rngal," she said.

"I can't exactly whisk her here."

Gina spoke slowly, her analytical mind at work, "At the tech hub, I know that the working conditions are awful. They keep the workers in barracks on-site, and they work long hours in the factories to make those awful gambling machines. The workers are rarely allowed out of the compound. But there is the gauntlet project. If we are in charge and can work with Brtann and Lnore, we could change it." Gina was a little breathless thinking about how much work would be involved, but continued, "It needs a major overhaul, but not destruction. Rngal and I could do it."

Gina wanted to stay here, Montel thought. He said, "Ok Gina, then let's get you back to Rngal."

Gina almost fell over herself, "Yes!" Impulsively, she threw her arms around his neck in happiness. Montel hesitated, unsure how much of this affection was related to the phana. But then he gave in, gently wrapping his arms around Gina. Around the edges of clans Awakening and Sunnico's collapse, their relationship had shifted. Gina had taken a first step to tentatively explore what this might mean.

73

Mendani, Rowan

Rowan opened his eyes. He was in a dark room. He sat up quickly but regretted it immediately, his head started ringing. He brought his hand to his head and could feel the dent that Hunter had made.

He nearly lay down again to stop the room from spinning, but he pushed through it. He felt his way to the door. He opened it and had to grit his teeth again. Light flooded in and felt like a thousand needles in his brain. He staggered backwards a few steps and leaned against a wall until the room stopped spinning.

A shadow darkened the doorway. "You've slept it off, have you?" Vraya's voice seemed to be booming into his ears.

"Geez Vraya, I'm right here, you don't need to yell."

Vraya laughed. Rowan clutched his pounding head. "Where are we?"

"I brought us to Mendani. Hunter unleashed his powers in Redall, he destroyed half the city and left with the elf. The only way I can understand it is that he's working with them now. I brought you with me back to Thaedim, we're at my house. You can decide what you want to do next."

Rowan's aching head was spinning for a new reason. "Hunter's gone?"

74

Prancinia, Montel

A few days later, Hunter was back to normal, he and Robyn started training again. Montel saw this as strange, but Gina assured him that it was normal mother-son bonding for them.

After one especially vicious bout of training, Hunter started to glow, and blue flames shimmered around him. Robyn kept sparring, goading him. Until he let off an uncontrolled blast in her direction.

"Mom!" Hunter shouted

Robyn didn't dodge but let the flames hit her. Her innate resistance to heat protected her. Unfortunately, the walls in Montel's garden did not have similar protective features.

"What was that?!" Montel yelled from a window on the ground floor when he saw the rubble. "That's it, no more training here. Need I remind you that we are trying to keep a low profile?"

"I couldn't agree more." Robyn called back to him. Turning to her son. "Hunter, you need to learn how to control your power. We're going back to Thaedim."

Montel nodded; this was good.

Gina appeared at an upstairs window, after hearing the explosion and saw the destruction. "Hunter! What the hell? We want to live here, not destroy it!" Amazingly, Hunter looked sheepish. "Montel," Gina called down, "I'm so sorry!"

Both Robyn and Montel noticed Hunter's unguarded reaction.

Gina came downstairs and into the garden, yelling at Hunter and demanding to know what he'd done.

As Gina lectured Hunter on how clan magic was not meant for the destruction of private property, Montel and Robyn watched the interaction. Both becoming aware that this bond could be used to manipulate Hunter's power.

Robyn and Hunter started planning to leave Djania and head back to Thaedim. Montel sourced a small motorboat that could get them there if the weather held. They packed enough supplies to last a few weeks.

Hunter hugged Gina goodbye for a second time. He said quietly: "I know you'll always show up."

"I wouldn't have it any other way. See you next crisis," she replied softly.

75

Prancinia, Gina

As the small motorboat drifted into the distance, this time it was Gina waving Hunter off to his new adventure. When she couldn't see them anymore, she turned from the coast to look at Montel. His mind seemed to be elsewhere, eyes focused on the water, the lapping waves were drawing his attention. Gina was new to experiencing magic, her time since invoking the phana had not been long, but she could feel a quiet thrum hovering between Montel and the ocean. His clan had water magic, could the events of the past days have Awakened something in him? Before she could pursue that thought further, he seemed to feel Gina's stare, shook his head once as if to clear his thoughts, and turned to her.

"Shall we go see Rngal?" he asked, reaching for Gina's hand.

She nodded, "At last!"

As they drove toward the tech hub, Gina reflected on how many questions Montel must have about the phana after seeing it invoked for the first time, and by a non-breesian. He had not pressed her when she'd been evasive to his questions. Maybe she would be able to explain it clearly one day, but for now that was beyond her.

A short while later, they arrived at the Sunnico tech hub. The gates were closed until Gina got out of the car and showed herself to the guards. They were the same ones that had brought her in just a few weeks back. They let both her and Montel through.

Gina found her way to Rngal's office. The door was closed but Gina thundered through, bounding in towards Rngal.

Rngal managed to stand before Gina came crashing into her, almost barrelling Rngal over.

The air seemed to shimmer around them as the phana re-asserted itself, settling lightly over them and renewing the mental bond. It seemed that the formal rituals weren't needed once the spell was established.

"I'm back! And you won't believe what happened! All of Sunnico's power is gone in Redall, it was destroyed."

"Someone is welcome!" Rngal greeted her in the traditional way, then switched to Nülandish, "Brtann warned me something like this might happen when he sent the gauntlet specs here."

"Gauntlet specs? You mean the plans to develop the gauntlets are going ahead? What about the gambling machines?" Gina asked.

"It may not have seemed like it when we first arrived, but I've been staging a quiet coup since my return here. I've paused the construction of the gambling machines, shifting it to the gauntlets. We should have a first batch of gauntlets ready for testing in a few more weeks."

Gina's jaw was hanging open, "Well, it looks like you've sorted everything out."

"There's so much more to do. I want to change the working conditions for the factory staff and optimise the factory equipment. And then there's the roll out of the gauntlets. And then I need to figure out how to put a definitive end to the gambling production side."

"We're here to help, Montel and I, we want to make this change happen with you."

Both turned to look at Montel, who was waiting in the doorway.

CONCLUSION

Robyn and Hunter had spent nearly four days on the small motorboat. Hunter was beginning to wonder if taking off on a trip to Thaedim with his mom had really been the best option. But as the landmass emerged from the fog of their fourth morning on the water, Hunter knew he'd made the right decision. They came upon the northern coast of Thaedim, new territory for both, also only a few days' journey to Mendani. Hunter had insisted on stopping there to find out what had happened to Vraya and Rowan.

Robyn jumped out of the boat into the shallow water.

Like she'd done so many years before she pulled the boat in. This time knowing that a new adventure waited for her.

About the authors

A mother-son duo tackled the challenge National Novel-Writing Month in November 2023 and this book is the result.

Andrea Campbell

Born in Canada and having lived on three continents, Andrea works in political communications in the EU capital, Brussels. Her experience across cultures and languages has been a feature of her career and life so far. She looks forward to developing the Awakened universe, bringing in both the discord that happens when cultures clash and the beautiful collaboration when different cultures meet.

Haruto Iwasaki

Born in Belgium to Japanese and Canadian parents, Haruto has been a world traveller since birth. His day job is high school, and he is working towards being trilingual. His interest in anime and manga influenced his development of the Awakened universe.